Just Plain Pickled to Death

an amish bed and breakfast mystery with recipes #4

TAMAR MYERS

NYLA Publishing
350 7th Avenue, Suite 2003, NY 10001, New York.
http://www.nyliterary.com

Dedication

For Joseph Pittman, Senior Editor at Dutton Signet

ACKNOWLEDGEMENTS

I would like to acknowledge Eben Weiss, Assistant Editor at Dutton Signet, as well as the behind-the-scenes players there who are an in-valuable part of the team. Special thanks goes to Tom Longshaw of Rock Hill, who helped me when I was in a pickle. In addition, I would like to thank the Blue Stocking Club of Pittsburgh ("younz" are great), and the Blue Stocking Book Club of Rock Hill, South Carolina (thanks, y'all for the support).

1

Sarah Weaver was found dead in a barrel of pickled sauerkraut. On my back porch. Freni, who found her, screamed, fainted, and then screamed again. I merely fainted.

Aaron Miller, my fiance, slapped me gently back to consciousness.

"It's okay," he said. "Susannah is calling the police."

I raised up on one elbow and eyed the barrel balefully. "It's not okay," I wailed. "It's horrible!"

"What I meant is that the authorities have been called. It's still horrible about the body."

What I meant was that a perfectly good barrel of sauerkraut had been ruined, and I would be hard-pressed to find a replacement in time for my wedding supper just a week away. That was my gut reaction, but of course I didn't say that. Please don't get me wrong, it was horrible about the woman in the barrel too, but she was obviously very dead and there was nothing to be done about that now. Besides which, if that was who I thought it was, she had been missing for almost twenty years.

"Ooooh," Freni moaned. "Ooooh."

Aaron left my side to attend to my elderly cousin.

I got up on all fours, then on my knees, and took another quick peek at the woman I thought was Sarah Weaver. It was a morbid thing to do, but I felt strangely compelled. Besides which, somebody needed to make a positive identification.

As far as I could tell, it was her all right. Same long blond hair, same cheap plastic hair bands, same awful paisley dress. Still, pickling is not kind to one's features, and an autopsy was no doubt in order just to be a hundred percent sure.

A wave of nausea hit me like a ton of bricks, and I lay back down again and closed my eyes. I tried focusing on my special spot, which is a pond just across the road from my farm. That worked for a while, and although I could still hear Aaron's calm voice as he tried to soothe Freni, I was at least able to shut the picture of Sarah with sauerkraut in her hair out of my mind. At least until my sister, Susannah, came back.

"I called Melvin," she said, sounding just as normal as could be. "He and Zelda will be right over. He said not to touch anything. Especially not to eat any of the kraut, on account it might not be good anymore."

A second wave of nausea hit me. "Call Doc Shafor," I managed to say through clenched teeth.

"Ah, do I have to?"

I pounded the porch floor with a fist, which Susannah correctly interpreted as a command. She left whining, and I lay still for a few minutes before crawling off into the house to collect my thoughts. That took several minutes more.

Sarah Weaver, I remembered, was not the only member of her family to go missing for two decades.

Her mother, Rebecca Weaver, had disappeared approximately a month before her daughter had. Perhaps she was in that barrel as well. I forced myself to glance at the barrel again. No, Sarah's mother couldn't possibly be sharing the same slatted coffin. There simply wasn't enough room. At least she hadn't shown up on my back porch the week of my wedding.

I started to breathe a sigh of relief, and then I remembered something else. It was obvious that Aaron hadn't recognized Sarah. Perhaps he should have. Aaron and Sarah were first cousins, after all. Sarah's mother, Rebecca—the first to go missing—was Aaron's aunt, his father's sister. But in all fairness, Aaron had left Hernia, Pennsylvania, when his cousin was only nine or ten.

I'm afraid that now is the time to confess that the reason my fiance left home was to join the army. That was in 1972, and the Vietnam War was still in progress. The very fact that Aaron volunteered to fight in a war literally broke his parents' hearts. His mother actually died the following year.

You see, Aaron and Sarah, like my sister, Susannah, and I, were raised Amish-Mennonites. Our pacifist roots go back to 1536, to a man named Menno Simons (from whom we get the word "Mennonite"). They were slightly modified in 1693 by a man named Jakob Amman (from whom we get the word "Amish") and brought to this country in 1738 by our ancestor Jacob Hochstetler and his contemporaries. My particular branch of the family tree curved back on itself and became Mennonite again, while other closely related branches remained staunchly Amish.

From this brief description of my ancestors you may extrapolate two things. The first is that despite their resistance to military service, the Mennonites, Amish, and Amish-Mennonites are longtime Americans and loyal to the core. The second is that my forebears are more interbred than pedigreed poodles, and only slightly less interbred than the royal families of Europe. To put it bluntly, I am my own cousin. Several times over.

The upshot is that Aaron and I are somehow cousins, but not so closely related that we can't be legally married. Of course, Sarah Weaver—the unfortunate young woman in the sauerkraut barrel—was some sort of a cousin to me as well, but she was Aaron's first cousin. I was going to have to tell him that, since he obviously didn't remember her.

Aaron would undoubtedly be stunned at first, but he hadn't known his cousin well enough to be grief-stricken. Susannah had. Sarah and Susannah had been best girlhood friends until that tragic day—it was around the Fourth of July, if I remember right— when Sarah Weaver disappeared. Her disappearance had rocked the town of Hernia and, indeed, a large portion of the state. A massive hunt, involving dogs and even the FBI, ensued, but of course the girl had never been found. For some reason my sister's mind had been unable to cope with the loss of her best friend, and so she simply didn't. That's what it seemed like, at any rate. One day Sarah and Susannah were giggling about boys, and the next day Susannah was giggling alone. It was as if Sarah had never existed.

Mennonites of our ilk don't put much stock in psychotherapy—we rely on the Bible instead—but even that wasn't enough to make Susannah face reality.

Unfortunately, my poor sister might have to face the truth in just a matter of minutes because Melvin, our chief of police, had all the sensitivity of a bull in heat, and Melvin would undoubtedly recognize Sarah. The two of them had once dated in high school.

I found Susannah waiting on the front porch for Melvin and Zelda to show up. Susannah had dated Melvin too— much more recently, in fact—but even though she no longer cared an owl's hoot for him, she couldn't stand to see him "in the clutches of Zelda."

"You all right?" I asked, sitting down next to her, on an Adirondack rocker.

"Fine," Susannah said impatiently, "but when that damn bitch gets here, I'm going to give her what for. Last time I saw her she was wearing a sweater I left in Melvin's car."

I hoped the sweater was cardigan and meant to be shed. My sister, despite her strict upbringing, has all the morals of the aforementioned bull in heat. She is ten years my junior, and when our parents died an untimely death in the Allegheny Tunnel, they inadvertently heaped a lot on my plate. Not only was I suddenly responsible for a very irresponsible sibling, but I was the owner of a farm as well. I was good at managing neither, and my sister ended up marrying and then divorcing a Presbyterian! The farm was downsized considerably and eventually became a very successful inn—the PennDutch—with a list of highfalutin clients like you wouldn't believe. Some of them are so highfalutin, in fact, that they have only first names.

"Susannah, dear," I said patiently, despite the fact that I don't tolerate swearing in my presence, "there is something I need to tell you before Melvin and Zelda get here."

"If you mean that story going around about the two of them getting married this fall, well, don't believe it. Melvin would rather read a book than marry her."

That described Melvin perfectly. The man would have you believe he's an animated version of the Encyclopaedia Britannica, but the only covers he's cracked are the ones on his bed. His arrogance is surpassed only by his stupidity. I know, it is unkind of me to talk this way, but how else can I describe a grown man who once mailed a gallon of ice cream—by UPS—to a favorite relative in another state?

"This has nothing to do with Melvin and Zelda, dear. It has to do with you. You and Sarah Weaver."

Susan's face had turned to stone. I knew she could no longer hear me, but I had to continue.

"I think that's Sarah Weaver back there," I said gently.

She said nothing. It was time to try another tack.

"You saw the girl in the barrel. Who do you think it is?"

Susannah and her stone face hopped off the porch and disappeared down Hertzler Lane just minutes before Melvin and Zelda arrived. I was tempted to go after her, but I know my sister, and I knew that she would be all right—in a manner of speaking. Sarah Weaver, and the barrel of kraut, had been left far behind.

2

I barely had time to tell Aaron that Sarah was his cousin before Melvin and Zelda came screeching up in a pathetic portrayal of proper police procedure. There was no need for them to have the siren wailing and the lights flashing, and there was certainly no need for them to jump out of the car with their guns drawn. Whoever killed Sarah Weaver had long since departed the scene, if not the earth.

"Put those things away," I chided them, and rightfully so. Both of them are distant kin as well, which means they have Amish forebears and therefore have no business handling weapons of any sort in the first place. Beyond that, anything in Melvin's hands makes him armed and dangerous. He almost put out his own eye with a weenie-roasting stick when we were kids, and it had a hot dog firmly attached to the end.

"Police business," Melvin said brusquely and tried to brush me aside.

I blocked his way.

"Just hold your horses, buster. The body in the barrel isn't going anywhere, and neither is the person who put her there."

"Oh, yeah? Says who?"

"Says me."

Melvin's left eye rotated slowly in its socket until it fixed on the right side of my face.

"Just who the hell do you think you are?"

"Magdalena Portulaca Yoder. I have brown hair, blue eyes, and am on the tall side. My current weight is none of your business. Neither is my age, except that you have it written down somewhere and you always get it wrong. I'm forty-four years old, Melvin, not fifty-four."

He made another unsuccessful attempt to stare at me. Melvin has bulging eyes that operate independently of each other, only one of several features that make him look like a giant praying mantis. Freni claims that Melvin was kicked in the head by a bull he tried to milk, which would explain one of the concave curves of his face. Others have told me that story as well. Personally, I'm inclined to believe that what you see is what you get. More than once I've come real close to pointing a can of Raid at Melvin to see his reaction.

"Move aside, Yoder!"

"Not until you put those awful guns away and hear me out."

"Aha! So you're obstructing justice, are you?"

Zelda stepped between the two of us. "We are just trying to do our job, Magdalena."

I looked over her head to Melvin. Now the right eye had locked in on the left side of my face, which is just as well, because it is my more flattering side.

"I have no interest in obstructing justice, Melvin. In fact, I have some information that may well speed up the process."

"Is this a confession?"

I prayed silently for patience to deal with Melvin. While I was at it, I prayed that I would win the Publishers Clearing House Sweepstakes. So far, neither prayer has been answered.

"I'll take your silence as a yes," Melvin sneered. "And don't think it comes as a surprise. You always were a violent one, Magdalena."

I took a solid step forward, forcing little Zelda to duck out of the way.

"You take that back, buster!"

I don't remember actually touching Melvin. I concede that I may have given him a gentle rap or two on the chest with my knuckles, but I certainly didn't mean him any bodily harm.

"Aha! Now it's assault!"

I stepped back. "What?"

There was a triumphant gleam in his eyes. Well, the right one, at any rate.

"You just added 'assaulting an officer' to the charges."

"What!"

"And you needn't shout, unless you want 'disturbing the peace' added to the list."

"It's Sarah Weaver," I screamed. "She's the one Freni found in the barrel of kraut on my back porch, and by the look of things, she's been in there an awfully long time. Probably since the day she went missing!"

Melvin's eyes jerked into temporary alignment. "My Sarah Weaver? The one I dated in high school?"

"The very one. And it was only one date, dear," I pointed out kindly. To have heard Sarah back then, it was one date too many.

"Sarah was never good enough for you anyway," Zelda muttered. To be truthful, I couldn't hear all the words clearly, but I'm sure that's the gist of what she said. Zelda Root not only has the hots for her boss, Melvin, but it's common knowledge that she is intensely jealous of anyone who normally sits down to micturate. No one in the community can convince her that—at least in this case—jealousy is a wasted emotion.

9

It was the left eye now, fixed on my nose. "You didn't like Sarah Weaver much, did you, Magdalena?"

"I liked her just fine." It was the truth. In fact, I probably liked her better than I did my sister back then.

"It's one thing not to like someone, Magdalena, but murder?"

"I did not murder Sarah Weaver!"

"Well, somebody did." Zelda had the irritating habit of butting into all my important conversations. "Teenage girls don't climb into sauerkraut barrels of their own accord."

"Well, even if this one did, she didn't do it on my back porch. That barrel was delivered just this morning."

"Oh?" They both said. They both sounded disappointed as well.

"That's right. Aaron Miller—my fiance—delivered that this morning. It was a wedding present from his father."

"Oh?" They were both interested again.

I stamped my foot. If big is beautiful, my feet are gorgeous. I stamped loud enough to scare away a crow that had been eavesdropping on the telephone line.

"See here! My Aaron isn't guilty, and neither is his father. That barrel had been sitting around in his root cellar since who-knows-when. Twenty years at least. When Aaron Senior heard that I was serving sauerkraut at my wedding supper, he sent it over as a gift."

Zelda made the kind of face I used to make when Mama fed me castor oil. As for Melvin, it is hard to tell when he makes faces.

"Ugh," Zelda said. "What kind of present is twenty-year-old sauerkraut?"

I shrugged. She had a point. Good sauerkraut can be made in a couple of months. And frankly, I had been bitterly disappointed when the two Aarons unloaded the barrel that morning. I had been hoping for a new clothes dryer—one of my recent guests had deposited a wad of gum the size of my fist in the inn's dryer, and I was having an awful time getting it all out.

"Aaron Senior grew up during the Great Depression," I said, trying to be loyal. "Folks who've lived through that don't throw anything away."

Zelda nodded. "My grandmother saves all her used tea bags. She claims they make good mulch for roses, only she hasn't grown roses for as long as I can remember. She must have over a thousand used tea bags in a big canister under the basement stairs."

Melvin snorted. "Well, I'm not buying this frugal bit. If that barrel came from the Miller farm, I'd say that makes Aaron Senior a prime suspect."

I forced myself to swallow my rage. If anger had calories, I would have blown up like a balloon. "Look, my Aaron was in Vietnam then, but if his father did it, why would he deposit the incriminating evidence on my back porch?"

"Some people can be awfully stupid," Melvin had the nerve to say.

I gained a few more imaginary pounds but managed to hold my tongue.

"And there is the issue of familiarity," Zelda said placidly. "Aaron Senior was Sarah's uncle, and most murderers know their victims, you know."

I whirled. "People in glass houses shouldn't throw stones, dear."

"What?" followed by "What?"

I addressed the soprano exclamation.

"I mean, who was dating Sarah back then? Melvin, right?"

"It was only one date. You said so yourself."

"One date—that I know of. Maybe there were more. Maybe Melvin tried to put the moves on her. Maybe she resisted. Maybe—"

"That's ridiculous!"

I glanced at Melvin, who was as white as a sheet got back in the days when Mama used to boil hers in borax.

"Maybe none of us should jump to conclusions," I said softly.

There were no more accusations that day.

"Call her father, dear," I said to Aaron after everyone had left.

"Can't."

"What do you mean you can't?"

"I don't know where he is, that's why."

"Then ask your father. He'll know. He knows—"

"Pops doesn't know either. Nobody does."

"What?"

"Uncle Jonas moved out of Hernia the summer following Sarah's disappearance. He never wrote, and he never called."

"Not anyone?"

"Not a soul. Uncle Jonas was a strange man, Magdalena, even before that terrible summer. Then his wife disappeared and, only a month after that, their daughter. It put him over the edge."

I tried to recall a face, but I have trouble keeping track of my own relatives. Undoubtedly one could populate a small nation with lost kinfolk of mine.

"Well, then, turn the job over to Melvin. He might as well do something useful."

"I already spoke to him about it when you were inside getting cold drinks. He doesn't think he'll have any luck either. Says he wants to put Pops down as next of kin."

I shuddered. Jonas's absence seemed somehow to add to the horror of the situation. Poor Sarah had been hanging around for twenty years in a barrel of kraut. She had a right to be buried with her father in attendance.

"They're all coming for the funeral," Aaron said. "They'll be here as fast as they can."

"Who's coming?" I asked. Whoever it was had better not want any supper. Freni had gone home as soon as the police left, and since there were no guests at the inn—on account of my upcoming wedding—I hadn't bothered to cook that evening. Neither Aaron nor I was hungry, and Susannah had yet to come home.

"The Beeftrust," Aaron said.

"Pooky Bear, we're having ham at the wedding, remember? And ribs to go with the kraut. Sorry, dear. We've gone over the menu a million times."

Aaron laughed. My beloved is breathtakingly handsome, with black hair, bright-blue eyes, and incredibly white teeth. When he laughs you can see every single one of those shiny pearls.

"The Beeftrust is not a meat company. It's my aunts."

"Aaron!"

He laughed again. "That's what they call themselves. You remember how big they are, don't you?"

I shrugged. I hadn't seen Aaron's aunts for years. At one time they had all been neighbors, and then gradually they moved out of Hernia, some of them to different states. In that time a lot of water had passed under my bridge. A lot of dirty water, and a lot of scalding water. Not much of it had been suitable for drinking.

"Well, I'm sure it will all come back to you when you see them. But be prepared, at any rate. Auntie Veronica is six two and two hundred pounds. I think she's the oldest."

I gulped. Visions of behemoth Millers were indeed coming back to me. Eveningmares, more than visions. None of the aunties—that I could remember— was fat, but they were all huge. Beefy, I guess, was the perfect way to describe them, although they possessed other physical peculiarities as well.

"Ah, yes, your aunt Veronica. She's the one with the—uh, uh, preposterous proboscis," I posed politely.

My Pooky Bear winced, and I felt ashamed. It wasn't true that Auntie Veronica's schnoz required its own Zip Code, no matter what folks said.

"Well, tell me about your aunt Leah," I said by way of deflection.

"Auntie Leah is the next oldest, and she's the tallest. She's six four, and she looks just like you."

"I'm five ten," I said pleasantly through gritted teeth.

"Oh, I meant her face. You two look enough alike to be related."

"We probably are related somehow, but let's hope she looks older."

"Yes, of course, that's what I meant. Auntie Lizzie, however, looks nothing like you. People say she looks English."

"Thanks." I wasn't sure what Aaron meant by that. When an Amish man says someone looks English, he means they look worldly. But Aaron, who had seen the world, could have meant anything.

"Auntie Lizzie always had the most incredible skin. Peaches and cream, Mama called it."

I bit my tongue. It wouldn't do to snap at my Pooky Bear so close to the wedding.

"Auntie Rebecca is, of course, still missing. She was the shortest of my aunties. Only a scant six feet in her stockings."

"Wasn't she the crabby one?"

"No, that's Auntie Veronica. But you would be crabby too if you had a nose like that," he added defensively.

It was time to change the subject. Believe it or not, a few of my detractors claim that I am crabby— mean-spirited, they have called me. And while my schnoz wasn't worthy of its own Zip Code, a P.O. box was not out of the question.

"Don't all your aunties have children? And aren't they coming as well?"

Aaron laughed heartily. "Of course they have children, but they're all grown now and have children of their own. Anyway, don't worry about that, because my cousins are too busy being moms and dads to come to a funeral and a wedding. I guess the good news is that they've all chosen the wedding."

That would have been good news, had I any sauerkraut to serve. "Well, what about the uncles? Are they coming for the funeral?"

"Yes, to the man. I hope you don't mind, honey, but I told them it would be all right to stay here. At the inn."

My Pooky Bear had just handed me a two-edged sword. It was the first time he had ever called me honey, and I wanted to leap for joy. Maybe even click my heels together and then leap again. But I didn't want company!

It had been no easy feat clearing the PennDutch Inn for my wedding. Bill and Hillary had been very polite about it, but I had to give the bum's rush to you-know-who. And as for the Hollywood crowd, if that woman ever slaps me again, I'm calling the cops.

My point is, it was at great sacrifice to my wallet that I had opened up the full calendar week leading up to my wedding.

I needed that time. That was time meant for me to prepare myself, both physically and psychologically, for my impending nuptials.

Believe me, it is no easy thing, getting married— even to someone as drop-dead gorgeous as Aaron. And I don't mean all the food preparations and such. Or the horrendous experience of trying to find a dress that is perfect. I'm talking about the institution itself, the irrevocable tying together of two human beings via the bonds of matrimony. It was especially difficult at age forty-four.

Sex would be too, I imagined. Of course I was a virgin. And no, I don't count that one time I accidentally sat on the washing machine during the spin cycle. My point is, I had a lot to think about, and the Beeftrust and their husbands were not on my schedule.

I smiled coyly at my Pooky Bear. "Can't your aunties stay at your house, dear? I mean, they are your father's sisters."

"Papa hasn't been feeling all that well, as you know, and anyway, you know how it is with two bachelors. The place is a mess."

I smiled. It is much easier being patient with Aaron than with Melvin, but nonetheless, it isn't always a piece of cake.

"Well, dear, your aunties were going to stay in motels for the wedding—what's a few extra days going to hurt? And isn't one of them so rich she just took a month-long cruise?"

Even before he opened his mouth, I realized I shouldn't have said it. Some people think of motels as being cold, impersonal places, and, alas, my Pooky Bear was one of them.

"These are my aunties, honey. I can't do that to them."

Well, he had just done it to me again. Slipped me the "honey" word when the going got tough.

"In that case, I'd be tickled to death to have them here," my lips said of their own volition.

As Julius Caesar might have said, let the games begin.

3

Aunt Veronica Gerber arrived later that same evening. She lives in Fox Chapel, a suburban community to the northeast of Pittsburgh, about a two-hour drive from here. Rumor has it that the maids in Fox Chapel have their own maids, and the Rolls-Royce that rolled up did nothing to dispel such idle gossip.

I hate to be cruel, but her nose was by far the first thing through the door. The rest of her followed presently, encased in a full-length mink coat. Given the fact that it was a warm spring evening, even the minks were sweating.

"Welcome!" I cried. I tried flinging my arms around her, like Aaron had done, but Aunt Veronica would have none of that from me.

"You would think the Pennsylvania Department of Transportation would do a better job of marking these back roads. We've been driving in circles for hours."

I stifled my impulse to remind her that she'd grown up here and should know these roads as well as she knows the spider veins on her nose.

"Have you eaten supper yet?" I asked graciously.

She stared down that long spidery nose at me.

"Goodness, child, you couldn't possibly expect us to be interested in food at a time like this."

I peered around the dead minks, looking for the other half of "we" and "us." Sure enough, she did have someone with her, a pudgy man, short (compared to her), who had silver hair and silver-rimmed glasses. Except for the Armani suit and five-hundred- dollar tie he was wearing, he would have blended in with any crowd of men in his age group. That is, if you didn't look too closely at the eyes behind the silver glasses: they were mere slits. I'd seen newborn kittens with larger pupils.

"Your chauffeur?" I asked politely.

"My husband, Rudy," she snapped.

"Uncle Rudy!" I extended my hand.

The slits closed, and then opened. Then ignoring my hand, he flung his arms around me and clasped me in the tightest embrace I have ever known. The sharp rims of his glasses dug into my bosom, meager as it is.

"Prepared to die, buster?" I mumbled over the top of his head.

He released me and began fiddling with that expensive tie.

"An apology would be nice," I said pleasantly.

"Magdalena!" Aaron said sharply.

For my Pooky Bear's sake I forced back my anger and with the utmost dignity led the way to the parlor. After we had settled them into the most comfortable chairs, Aaron and I attempted a few minutes of consoling conversation. Uncle Rudy said virtually nothing. Aunt Veronica, however, took every opportunity to preempt us with her acquired Fox Chapel accent.

Finally she just stood up. "Well, I don't know about younz's, but my feet are killing me, and I need to get to bed."

I glanced down to see the tiniest feet imaginable on a six-foot-plus woman. In their miniature black leather pumps they were like little round hooves. Tipping her over would be easier than tipping a sleeping cow. Not that I've done much of the latter, mind you.

"Right this way," I said graciously. I began leading the way up the quaint, winding stairs that my inn is so famous for.

"Not on your life, child!"

I looked down to see that although Rudy and Aaron were behind me, Veronica hadn't budged.

"There are back stairs," I called kindly. "But it's a fire escape, perhaps a mite too steep."

"The thing you're on is steeper than Jacob's ladder," she snapped. "Don't you have a room down here?"

"No, ma'am."

"Pssst," said Aaron through gleaming teeth.

I ignored him.

"What's this room back here that says Private on the door?"

"That's the storeroom," I said quickly. It was in fact a lie, and I would have been very ashamed of myself, except that in this case the lie really was told for a good cause. My bedroom, the only one downstairs, was filled with my wedding things. There was no use in getting her hopes up only to have them dashed.

Aunt Veronica must have picked up some terrible manners in Fox Chapel. My room wasn't locked, and so she barged right on in. I squeezed past Rudy and Aaron, but before I could reach the bottom of the stairs she had emerged with a triumphant smile on her face.

"I'll take this room," she announced.

"Over my dead body." I said it as calmly and lady-like as I could under the circumstances.

"Magdalena, please," Aaron whispered. "She is the oldest of the aunties."

"I don't care if she's Methuselah in drag," I said. "I'm not giving up my room."

"Sweetie, are you just going to stand there and let her talk to me that way?"

For a minute I thought she was talking to her husband, Rudy, but the woman was smarter than that. No doubt she had been the "sugar-auntie" of Aaron's childhood. The strings she was pulling were attached to memories of lollipops.

"Mags?"

I looked into Aaron's incredibly blue eyes and felt my resolve melting. If my Pooky Bear really wanted me to sacrifice not only my inn but my very room to the Beeftrust, so be it.

I took a deep breath. "Well—"

"Get on in here, Rudy, and give Big Mama a hand. There's junk spread all over this bed."

That did it. That hiked my hackles. The so-called junk was my bridal veil and an assortment of dried flowers from Mama's bouquet when she married Papa. I had been painstakingly sewing some of the flowers into the net of my veil when Freni opened the barrel.

"Step into my room again and you won't have a hoof left to stand on," I said sweetly. "Your room is upstairs, the last one on the left. If you look hard you may find a clean towel in the linen closet at the end of the hall. I was planning to wash the sheets tomorrow. I wasn't expecting guests, you know."

Aaron should have seen things my way, because I was, after all, his honey. His soon-to-be wife. I guess at that point, blood was still thicker than water, and Aunt Veronica shared more blood with him than I did. At any rate, he didn't say another word to me the rest of the evening. In fact, as soon as he had washed and dried the sheets for his precious auntie, he was out of there. I didn't see or hear from him until the next morning.

I was sound asleep dreaming that Aaron and I had reconciled and had just dived (with our clothes on!) into Miller's Pond, across the road from the PennDutch Inn, when the real-life PennDutch Inn got hit by a tornado. At least that's what it sounded like. Tornadoes, I'm told, sound like trains, and that's exactly what I heard as I swam up through the dream-thick waters of the pond and broke the surface of consciousness.

"Hit the cellar!" I yelled, rolling out of bed.

It appeared to be too late to take cover. The inn was shaking violently. At this point it was every woman for herself. You understand, of course, and I'm sure you would have rolled right under that bed the same as I did.

This tornado, however, possessed human lungs, and as full consciousness returned, I realized its vortex was located just outside the front door. The thing didn't quit howling until I'd let it in.

"Well, it's about time!"

My gaze wandered up and up until, just below the lowest cloud strata, it encountered a vaguely familiar visage. Despite Aaron's claims, she does not look like me. If indeed she ever did, then something terrible has happened to one of us.

Besides the fact that she is half a foot taller than I, and a good hundred pounds heavier, the woman has no neck. Zilch. Her smallish head sits directly on quarterback shoulders. At least I could wear a necklace, if I so desired. Maybe not a five-strand pearl collar, like Princess Di, but something. Perhaps the good Lord was being kind when he neglected to give Auntie Leah a neck; as it is, she passes through two climate zones.

"Aunt Leah! Come in," I said graciously.

The train hurtled into the lobby, nearly knocking me over. It was followed a few seconds later by the cutest little caboose.

"Uncle Solomon?"

I offered him my hand, which he took in both of his. I don't mean to be rude, but I've seen corn kernels almost as long as his fingers. The man was also bald as a cue ball and barely taller than a cue stick. Like Uncle Rudy, he wore a suit and a tie. Clearly it was a marriage made in heaven. Mere mortals could never have gotten them together.

"That's just terrible about our little Sarah," Auntie Leah boomed. "Do the police have any suspects?"

I shook my head, carefully avoiding eye contact with Aaron. "After all, the trail is twenty years old."

Uncle Solomon rubbed a pudgy little hand over his shiny dome. "I read the most interesting thing in the paper recently," he said. He spoke rapidly, as if he was afraid of being interrupted. "It happened in France. Someone found a body—a murder victim— in a cave high up in the Pyrenees. Apparently it was quite cold in the cave, and the body had been there for many years. It was perfectly preserved. The autopsy even revealed what the victim had eaten for breakfast and—"

"Speaking of breakfast," Auntie Leah bellowed, "what is for breakfast?"

"Breakfast?"

"Eggs and bacon would be nice," Uncle Solomon muttered. "And cinnamon toast. I love cinnamon toast."

Auntie Leah scowled at her husband. "The motel we stayed at just offered Continental breakfasts. It's no wonder the Europeans are so puny. English muffins and croissants—imagine that!"

"I hadn't thought about breakfast," I said calmly. "I'm not really open for business, you know. But there's some cereal boxes in the kitchen cupboard next to the refrigerator. You're welcome to help yourselves."

"Cereal?" Leah barked. "You want us to eat cereal? Why, I never! In my day we served our company real meals—ham, bacon, sausage, eggs, pancakes, waffles, fried potatoes. You name it. I got up before dawn to put my best foot forward."

I glanced down at her feet. Thankfully, they were of normal size, and she wouldn't be demanding my bed.

"Be my guest, dear. The kitchen is that way. For your information, I like my eggs poached, and my bacon with a little play left in it. Before you start you might want to run upstairs to room six to see what Auntie Veronica and Uncle Rudy want."

"Veronica is here?"

"You don't think the Rolls-Royce is mine, do you, dear?" I could be persuaded to like this woman.

"It's a beautiful Rolls," Uncle Solomon said agree-ably. "I'm particularly fond of the classic Phantom series—"

"You mean she spent the night?" Auntie Leah bawled.

"She snored like a hibernating bear. Kept me awake until the wee hours this morning." Actually, the fact that Susannah hadn't returned yet was what had done it, but I wasn't about to confide in a stranger.

"The nerve of that woman!"

"You're telling me!"

"She always has to be first, you know. First to be born, first to—"

" 'And the first shall be last,' " I said, quoting Scripture.

"—move out of Hernia, first to buy a genuine ranch house, first to get a television. Whenever there's a wedding or a funeral, that woman just has to be the first to get there. It's like a convulsion or something."

"I think you mean 'compulsion,' dear," I said kindly.

"Whatever! Is there nothing that Veronica hasn't done first?"

"She has yet to cook a meal in my kitchen," I said hopefully.

"Well, I'll soon fix that."

She chugged off, like a train on a trestle, trailing her reluctant caboose. Fortunately I had dusted the doorway lintels for cobwebs just the day before.

I had decided to wait for my breakfast in the comfort of my bed and was headed back to my room when the front door slammed open. I turned to see my sister, Susannah, flow in. I mean that literally. It's not that Susannah, is particularly graceful, mind you, it's just that her usual attire is fifteen yards (give or take a foot) of frothy fabric.

This morning Susannah was wearing a lavender print chiffon that, if memory served me, was the same stuff she'd had on the day before. It also looked more than a little worse for wear, and I could only hope those were ketchup stains I saw settle into place.

"Susannah!"

"Oh, Mags, don't you even think about starting in on me. I've had one hell of a rough night."

"We don't swear in this house, do we, dear," I reminded her gently.

Susannah rolled her eyes so high that for a second only the whites could be seen. "A couple of pews and an offering plate and we could rename this joint Saint Magdalena's Church. There is one with that name in Pittsburgh, you know."

"Is that where you were, dear? In Pittsburgh? Did you visit Mystery Lovers Bookshop?"

Susannah doesn't have a car, and she hadn't taken mine, but I knew that was no obstacle. That girl gets around more places than the postal truck.

"You think I went to Pittsburgh? I wish!" Susannah stamped a long, slender foot, and from deep within the settled swirls there came a faint bark.

In case you haven't heard, Susannah owns one of those rat-size dogs, and she carries it around in her bra (a gal has to put something in her bra, doesn't she?). Shnookums is the beast's name, and contrary to public opinion, I am not out to do the critter in. I mean only to stand my own ground, which is not easy to do in this case, even though the dog weighs only two pounds soaking wet. That's because this cantankerous cur is fifty percent teeth, and fifty percent sphincter muscle. No matter from which direction you approach the mutt, you're bound to lose.

"Well, where did you go?"

"Johnstown."

"Johnstown is nice. The incline railway is especially interesting. The steepest car-carrying one in the world, I believe."

"I didn't ride the incline, Mags. I had a date."

I nodded to show that I understood, although I hadn't a clue what was going on. Aaron and I had a wonderful date riding up and down the Johnstown incline.

"Of course, only half of them showed up," she added.

"Only half your date showed up?" Thankfully I had more sense than to ask which half. In the old days it might have been a joke. But from what Susannah tells me about the TV talk shows she watches, this could well be a serious question.

"Yeah," she said disgustedly. "The pitcher was there, and so was the shortstop. The first and second basemen came late. The catcher didn't stop by until almost the end, and I never did see the third baseman." She stomped her foot again, and Shnookums howled on cue. "Or half the outfield, for that matter."

"You dated a softball team?"

Her eyes rolled back until they challenged gravity. "Really, Mags, how dumb can you get? It was a baseball team."

I said a quick but fervent prayer of thanksgiving. I didn't approve of my sister's behavior, mind you, but I was overjoyed that she was her normal self again. I had been afraid that her abrupt brush with reality the day before might have altered her equilibrium. I realized, of course, that it was important for Susannah to seek professional help, but since she'd managed to avoid it for twenty years, what harm was one or two more weeks going to do?

As soon as Aaron and I got back from our honeymoon I was going to see to it that Susannah got the help she needed. It might take both Aaron and me, along with a team of horses, to do it, and undoubtedly Susannah would hate me for the rest of her life, but it had to be done. After my wedding!

4

My Pooky Bear showed up just in time for breakfast, and it was immediately clear that all was forgiven. The humongous bouquet of freshly picked irises he thrust at me would have been proof enough.

The kiss that followed scorched my lips to the gums. I will confide here that it was only our second kiss—we Mennonites tend to be chaste. I shudder to think what might have transpired had we been Presbyterians like Susannah.

"I see that Auntie Leah has arrived," he said jovially.

"How can you tell?"

"The New Jersey plates. My guess is that the next one to show up will be Auntie Lizzie. I know she lives in Pennsylvania—but it's all back roads from Du Bois to here, and neither she nor Uncle Manasses will drive at night. Otherwise she would have been the first to arrive."

Aaron was absolutely right. I had just devoured my bacon—not quite enough play but still good—when the Du Bois duo danced in. I don't mean that literally, since Aunt Lizzie Blough is a devout Mennonite, but still, she and Uncle Manasses are by far the most liberal members of our sect I have encountered. They almost look English!

True, Auntie Veronica and Uncle Rudy are wealthy enough to put your average Episcopalian to shame, but from the neck up they look like Mennonites. Not that all Mennonites have big noses, mind you. What I mean is that Auntie Veronica does not wear makeup, and her jewelry is confined to that ten-carat monstrosity on her left ring finger. As for Uncle Rudy, although I had yet to see his teeth, undoubtedly they were the only place he wore gold. If you stuck the two of them in the right clothes and put them in a buggy, they could pass for Amish in the eyes of a tourist. Not so for the Du Bois duo.

"Can you believe it? Platinum-blond hair?" I whispered to Susannah.

"Cool," my pseudo-pagan sister cooed.

"And lipstick?"

"But it's pale," Susannah sniffed, immediately relegating Aunt Lizzie to the ranks of minor apostates.

"And pierced ears?" I almost shrieked.

Actually, it was more amazing than appalling that the woman had ornaments dangling from her ears. They were, without a doubt, the smallest ears I'd ever seen on an adult human being. They were like tiny dried apricots, but of course not so orange. I checked her feet quickly; they were normal. Her hands, however, were not. She could have spanned an octave on a piano without even trying, two if she taxed herself at all.

Uncle Manasses was as much of a Mennonite anomaly as his wife. He was wearing a suit and a tie, but his was a bolo tie, with a turquoise steer skull as the slide. Both his hair and his mustache owed their pigmentation to a drugstore bottle. These manifestations of the world's influence were disconcerting, but it was the distinct outline of a cigarette pack in his pocket that was shocking.

Sure, Susannah smokes, but she is ten years younger than I am and of a generation totally lost. Uncle Manasses is the age my father would have been had he not ended his life sandwiched between an Adidas truck and a milk tanker. Papa would sooner have danced naked with the Lennon Sisters than let one of the devil's toothpicks touch his lips. It was clear to me that the Bloughs were borderline Presbyterians, and well on their way to becoming Episcopalians if someone didn't turn them around.

"Oh, that's just so terrible about little Sarah," Auntie Lizzie said to each of us, as she hugged us in turn.

I could smell the world on Aaron's auntie. It smelled like the perfume counter at J. C. Penney.

"Yes, terrible," Uncle Manasses murmured, but he didn't sound convinced.

Then again, poor Sarah had gone missing—and was presumed dead—twenty years before. It is hard to maintain grief that long, and unless you have a body in a barrel to jolt your memory, it is hard to recapture grief that is two decades old.

"Well, the Lord giveth and the Lord taketh away," Aunt Lizzie said, patting a stray platinum puff back into place.

"Amen," Uncle Manasses said. He reached into his shirt pocket and pulled out a coffin nail.

"I don't allow smoking indoors," I said calmly.

Six pairs of eyes turned to stare at me. Susannah was the only one who snickered.

"Well, you know what the surgeon general says. Smoking is not only hazardous to your health but also to mine."

"Magdalena, please," Aaron begged, his voice barely a whisper.

Uncle Manasses regarded me with the same detachment I am used to receiving from Matilda and Bessie, my milk cows.

"A week of secondhand smoke isn't going to hurt you at all. I've been smoking for fifty years, and I'm fit as a fiddle."

I smiled pleasantly. "That may be, dear, but you smell like an ashtray. You want to smoke, then go outside. This is my house."

"Honey, he's my uncle."

It was the "H" word again, but I would not be swayed. "I don't care if he's the president of the United States. No one smokes in my house."

"You go, girl!"

Six pairs of eyes, including mine, turned to Aunt Lizzie. No one snickered.

Auntie Lizzie smoothed her perm, pleased with the attention.

"I've been telling Manasses the same thing ever since we got married, only he won't listen to me. But he has to listen to you." She swatted at the air with a hand reminiscent of a tennis racket. "Sometimes the smoke gets so thick I could cut it with a knife. I'm glad that finally somebody else has the moxie to stand up to him."

Thereafter, Auntie Lizzie and I became firm friends. But I'm afraid my standing up to Uncle Manasses put the strain back in my relationship with Aaron. Thanks to the aunties—and ultimately to Sarah in the kraut—the week preceding my wedding was not progressing as smoothly as I had planned.

Auntie Lizzie and I were just finishing up the dishes—Auntie Leah can cook, but you'd think she'd never seen a sponge—when the last of the Beeftrust appeared.

Auntie Magdalena arrived not with a bang but with a whimper. Who knows how long the woman had been standing there in the kitchen door, whimpering like a frightened puppy, before I turned and saw her.

"Auntie Magdalena Fike?"

"Yes. Who are you?"

"Magdalena Yoder. Aaron's fiancee."

The woman sighed a couple of times, whimpered something that I couldn't understand but that sounded like "Please pass the cheese," and then sighed again. Each time she sighed, the largest bosom I'd ever seen rose and fell like ocean waves after a storm. I don't mean to be indelicate here, but a brassiere that size could hold a full-grown cocker spaniel—though nothing else, of course.

"Is Uncle Elias here as well?" I asked pleasantly.

At the mention of his name Uncle Elias stepped smartly forward. Like the other uncles he was on the short side and dressed in a suit and a tie, but unlike them he was a very handsome man. He was also very black.

I confess that I was shocked, and even though she vigorously denies it, so was Susannah. The truth is, up until that moment, neither of us had ever seen a black Mennonite. Of course they exist—ours is not a closed denomination—but not in Hernia. I, for one, had never heard of a Hernia Mennonite marrying a black Mennonite.

The truth is, I was speechless.

"Did you get a chance to eat a proper breakfast?" Aunt Lizzie asked politely. Obviously she had seen Uncle Elias before.

The Fikes had come the farthest. From what I understood, they had flown into Pittsburgh from St. Louis, where they now lived, and then rented a car. From what I already knew about Aaron's aunties, nothing between the Pittsburgh airport and my Hernia would have sufficed for breakfast.

"Disjoint my head, then you're fired," Auntie Magdalena whimpered.

"Why, I never!" And I hadn't.

Uncle Elias smiled patiently. "What she said was, 'Just point me to a bed, I'm dead tired.'"

I pointed. But first I peeked at her feet to see if they could get her up the stairs without complaint. Except for the moss on her shoes they looked entirely normal. Apparently Auntie Magdalena was the exception to the Beeftrust rule. There was nothing about her that was in any way diminutive.

"Stanks," she whimpered after I'd shown them to their room and obligingly fluffed up the pillows.

As I was reaching for the two-dollar tip, I noticed that she had the tiniest hands imaginable on someone that large. Mere child's hands they were.

Thanks to my inn's popularity, the phone all but rings off the hook. I know, I should hire a full-time receptionist, but I refuse to, as long as Susannah is in residence. Freni Hostetler, who is in her seventies, does all the cooking, and I do everything else—except for the ALPO guests. Those folks elect to pay extra for the privilege of participating in the Amish Lifestyles Plan Option, and consequently they get to do their own laundry and maid service. Susannah, however, does nothing—at least nothing connected to running the inn. You would think that answering the phone wouldn't be too strenuous for her nails, but unless her personal radar informs her that an incoming call is from a virile male, the phone can ring its bell to a nub and she'll ignore it.

"PennDutch Inn, but I'm closed for business this week," I said crisply.

There was a lot of static on the line, but I was able to piece together enough words to ascertain that a Middle Eastern potentate wanted to rent the entire inn for himself and his harem.

"When?"

"Starting tomorrow. For a week."

"Sorry, no can do."

I was in the act of hanging up when I heard an obscene amount of money being offered.

"I beg your pardon? Would you mind saying that again?"

The static cackled the same obscene figure—more than ten times what I would make by renting out the PennDutch at my regular rates.

"Sorry, but a ragtag gathering of grotesque giantesses doth gyre and gimble in the wabe."

"Eh?"

"What I mean is, I've already got a full house," I said sadly. More static.

"No, there is not a casino attached to the inn. What I'm trying to say is that I have to turn your lucrative offer down on account of my soon-to-be-husband's aunties have taken over the place."

Before I hung up I accepted an offer from him for twice as much money as his previous one, but for the following week instead. In the meantime the persistent potentate was going to purchase a small New Jersey town in which to stash his happy harem.

The receiver was in its cradle for exactly three seconds before the phone rang again.

"Oh second thought," I said smoothly, "I think a deposit of ten thousand is in order."

There was silence instead of static.

"I mean, what if your ladies decide to make veils out of my curtains?"

"Magdalena? Have you gone totally off your rocker?"

"Melvin? Melvin Stoltzfus?"

"That's Chief of Police Stoltzfus to you. And what the hell kind of game are you playing?"

Thank the good Lord I don't own one of those newfangled telephones that shows your picture on a screen. Undoubtedly I was three shades darker than pickled beets.

"Why did you call, Melvin?" I asked evenly.

"Oh, that. I called to officially inform you that Sarah Weaver is dead."

I am not surprised by anything Melvin can say. Which is not to say I'm never dismayed.

"Is there a point to this, Melvin?"

"I just got the coroner's report back, and like I said, Sarah Weaver is definitely dead."

"I see." What else could I say?

"And she's been dead a long time."

"You don't say. Anything else?"

"It was murder."

"That crossed my mind too," I said. "Any idea as to how she died?"

"The coroner wants to send some tissue samples off to Harrisburg, but he's pretty sure the cause of death was a blow to the head. Possibly a hammer."

"That's it?"

"A blow to the head can be fatal, you know."

I bit my tongue.

"Where did you get that barrel of sauerkraut from, Magdalena?"

I put my hand over the speaker holes before sighing a long, deep sigh that would have made Magdalena Fike proud.

"I already told you, Melvin, so I'm only going to tell you once more. The sauerkraut was a gift from Aaron's father. He'd had it in the back of his root cellar for years and finally decided to get rid of it. He and Aaron brought it over yesterday morning. Freni is very particular about the kraut she serves, so she decided to give it a preview taste. After all, the barrel looked ancient. That's when she found the body."

"Was it in the barrel at the time?"

"No, Sarah had gotten out to take a brief stroll— Melvin!"

"I am being thorough, Magdalena. Asking as many questions as I can think of is part of my job."

"Then why don't you ask them of Aaron's father? He's the one who made the sauerkraut and then gave it to me as a gift twenty years too late."

I felt a sudden need to do a little whimpering of my own. What kind of family was I marrying into? The ideal father-in-law, I had imagined—when I was but a mere idealistic girl— would give brood sows and freshened heifers as gifts, not sauerkraut. Given enough time, I can make my own sauerkraut.

"I'm one step ahead of you, Magdalena," Melvin crowed triumphantly. "I plan to see old man Miller this afternoon."

It was my turn to crow. "No, you're not, dear. Aaron has taken his father into Bedford to buy him a new suit. If they can't find what they want there, then they're off to Somerset. At any rate, I don't expect them back until after supper."

Melvin said something that even Uncle Elias would have found difficult to decipher. After I made him repeat it four times I realized it was some sort of profanity and unless I wanted to risk undergoing an autopsy of my own, I was better off without a translation.

"You could come over tomorrow after church," I said graciously. "Papa Miller is going to be joining us for Sunday dinner."

He exploded with an expletive I recognized as one that Susannah used.

"Or why not just chat with him at the funeral luncheon on Monday? There is going to be a funeral, isn't there?"

"Don't count on it, Magdalena," he said, and to his credit, he said it without gloating. "Not by Monday. These things take time. This is a murder investigation, you know."

A blood-red flag had just been raised inches from my eyes. Fate was waving it tauntingly.

"I'm getting married a week from today, Melvin, after the funeral," I screamed.

Clearly it was going to be up to me to see that I did.

5

Magdalena Yoder's Wedding Feast, from Soup to Nuts

Great-Granny Yoder's Onion Cheese Soup
1 cup onions (finely chopped)
½ stick butter
¼ teaspoon salt
¼ teaspoon pepper
4 cups milk
2 tablespoons cornstarch
4 cups chicken broth
½ teaspoon dry mustard
2 cups shredded sharp cheddar cheese

Saute onions in butter, salt, and pepper until trans-parent. In measuring cup or small bowl, whisk together one-half cup of cold milk with the cornstarch. Pour mixture over onions, stirring constantly. Add chicken broth and remaining milk. Add dry mustard. Sprinkle shredded cheese over top while continuing to stir. Cook over low heat until the cheese is melted. Serve in bowls and garnish with croutons.

Serves 4.

6

Auntie Leah had decided to take a nap, so I was up to my elbows in sandwich fixings—trying desperately to get lunch on the table for the mass of milling, masticating Millers—when Freni finally showed up.

"I quit," she said.

"What?"

She threw down an apron that she hadn't even bothered to put on. "And you didn't even have the nerve to tell me!"

"Tell you what, dear?"

"Don't you give me the runaround, Magdalena Portulaca Yoder. I diapered you when you were a baby."

It was true. Besides my doctor, Freni is the only other living soul who has seen me naked. Not even Susannah has seen me in the buff. At Hernia High, because of the large concentration of Mennonites and other conservative folks, we didn't have to dress for gym.

Freni, who is Amish, is not only a kinswoman but a lifelong friend of the family. Prior to my parents' death, she and her husband, Mose, had both been employed on our farm. After Mama and Papa died they stayed on, and when I sold off most of the land and turned the farmhouse into a bed-and-breakfast inn, they became my staff. Mose tends the grounds and our two milk cows, and Freni cooks. They are long past retirement age but will not hear of it. Still, for reasons known only to her, Freni feels compelled to quit on a weekly—if not daily—basis.

I sat down on a kitchen chair that had been made by my great-grandfather. "Okay, Freni, spill it. What have I done to offend you this time?"

Freni's back stiffened. "Who said you offended me?"

"Don't I always manage to offend you?"

Freni whisked off her black traveling bonnet and patted the net prayer cap back into place over her coiled braids.

"You asked me to cook for your wedding, Magdalena—"

"I didn't ask, Freni. You offered. It was your wedding present."

"Yah, but you accepted, and that's the same thing."

I ignored her logic. After all, Freni thinks cheese is a vegetable. Enough said.

"What is the real reason, Freni? If it's because of Sarah, then I understand. Believe me, I can appreciate how much of a shock that was."

Freni tapped a black brogan impatiently. "It isn't Sarah—it's Barbara!" She was talking about her daughter-in-law.

That hiked my hackles for the second time in as many days. It was none of Freni's business who I chose to sing a solo at my wedding. I knew, of course, that Freni saw it differently. She comes as close to hating Barbara as the Bible will allow. Barbara's sin is that she is married to Freni's only child, John. That, and the fact that Barbara hails from the heathen hinterland of Iowa.

"Freni Hostetler! You should be ashamed of yourself. Poor Barbara has never done anything to hurt you."

Freni's eyes flashed volumes.

1 shrugged casually. "Well, then, I guess if you're not going to cook for my wedding, I'm just going to have to ask Auntie Leah. The breakfast she made this morning was simply delish."

"Leah Troyer?"

"The very one."

Freni looked as though I'd just slapped her. She pulled a chair out for herself and sat down heavily. Her breath was coming in irregular gasps.

"Of course, her cooking couldn't hold a candle to yours."

Her breathing became more regular.

"And the folks who are expecting a genuine Freni Hostetler feast will be disappointed."

Her breathing returned to normal, and a faint smile tugged at the corners of her mouth.

"You have quite a reputation hereabouts, you know," I said. It was the truth, depending on how you took it.

"And even in other states, yah?"

"Undoubtedly."

"Well, in that case I will have to do my duty, no matter now unfair some things may be." She cast me an accusing look.

"Duty above all else," I said charitably. "Now, how about you help me by finishing up these sandwiches while I go wake Auntie Leah? She's napping and asked for a twelve o'clock wake-up call."

Before I could get up, Freni leaned over and grabbed my left wrist. Despite her age, she has the grip of a sumo wrestler.

"You be careful of this bunch of Millers, Magdalena," she whispered. "They are a strange lot."

I sat back down. The sandwiches could dry out and Auntie Leah oversleep for all I cared.

"What do you mean, Freni? These people are Aaron's cousins."

She maintained the viselike grip. "Yah, they are his family, but he isn't like them. You can thank God for that."

"Freni!" I tried prying her fingers loose, but they were like bands of steel. "What is going on? What about the Millers?"

"Ach, where do I begin?"

"How about the beginning?"

Freni let go of my wrist, but her hand hovered above it, ready to pounce again if I tried to escape.

"How well do you remember the year Sarah Weaver disappeared?"

I shrugged. "Well, I was about twenty-six then. I think I remember it pretty well."

"Do you remember that her mama disappeared a month before she did?"

"Of course. At the time you told everyone that she had run off with the devil himself and was having a weekend of unbridled lust in the Poconos."

Freni glared at me. "Ach, how you twist my words. I said no such thing."

"Well, you did accuse her of hanky-panky with the accordion-playing evangelist who had come to town. Not all Baptists play that kind of drop-the- hanky, you know."

"I did see the two of them riding together in his truck," Freni snapped. "They could have been heading for the Poconos."

"We digress," I said pleasantly. "Tell me more about that summer. Wasn't it around the Fourth of July when Rebecca disappeared?"

Freni wrested control of the situation by waiting just until I opened my mouth to urge her on. "She ran off, like I said. And it was the end of July. The week of Aaron and Catherine's twenty-fifth wedding anniversary and—"

"Aaron and Catherine who?"

Freni stared at me like I had just spoken Japanese. "What?"

"Who were the Aaron and Catherine who were celebrating their twenty-fifth wedding anniversary?"

"Ach, have you lost your memory altogether, Magdalena? It was Aaron and Catherine Miller. Your Aaron's parents."

I laughed, albeit nervously. "It's your memory that's hit the skids, dear. If I was twenty-six, and my Aaron is the same age, then how could his parents have been celebrating their silver wedding anniversary?"

To her credit, Freni covered her mouth, so I only saw the tips of her smile. "Your Aaron was twenty-four that summer, not twenty-six. You were born the year a tornado took down Wagler Hooley's barn."

I felt my stomach fill with lead and sink to the floor. "You sure?"

"Positive. And Aaron was born two years later when we finally raised Wagler Hooley's new barn.

Wagler was so lazy, he wanted a whole year off from farming. Wouldn't let us build him a new barn any sooner."

She was at least right about the barn raising. Mama had gone into labor while helping to serve the community meal. Her water broke just as she was pouring the Amish bishop a glass of cider. Because Papa's car was blocked in by a sea of buggies, our Mennonite pastor drove Mama home, where I was born. I'd had to suffer through that story a million times.

Because there were two clergymen peripherally involved in my birth, Mama had declared that I would marry a man of the cloth. Instead, I was about to marry a man two years younger than I. A mere child. Perhaps Freni was right; perhaps I really was losing it. I should have remembered that although Aaron and I rode the same school bus, we were not in the same classes in high school. Somehow those two years had gotten lost among the intervening years in my memory.

"Tell Aaron how old I am and I'll tell your son everything you've ever said about his wife," I said kindly. I've made worse threats, if truth be told.

"Deal," Freni said quickly. "Now do you want to hear about that summer or no?" She barreled on anyway. "Well, Catherine had never been a very healthy woman, and no one thought she would live even that long, so it was an important occasion. The whole family was there to help celebrate, except for you- know-who."

"Aaron was in Vietnam," I reminded her.

She tossed her head at such a lame excuse. "Anyway, there was talk about bad feelings among some of the relatives."

"Which relatives? What sort of bad feelings?"

"Ach, do I get to tell the story or not?"

I hung my head in contrived shame. Years of experience had taught me how to appease the woman.

"The talk was that Rebecca's husband, Jonas, was jealous of one of the brothers-in-law. That Rebecca was paying too much attention to him and not to Jonas."

"Which of the brothers-in-law was that?"

"Ach, what does it matter now? It was that Baptist with the accordion that Rebecca had her eye on. After she ran off like that, and then Sarah disappeared, Catherine went down-hill fast. Blamed it on herself for having invited everyone to Hernia. She died the following winter." Freni looked at me accusingly. "Again no Aaron."

I returned her look. "By then Aaron was a prisoner of war in a bamboo cage a tenth the size of our chicken house."

Freni volleyed it right back at me. "Ach, the English and their strange ways. Volunteering to go to war."

"He would have been drafted anyway. He had a very low lottery number. And anyway, Aaron's not English, he's a Mennonite, as you well know." Of course, as a Mennonite, Aaron could have avoided the draft, but I wasn't going to remind her of that.

Freni rolled her eyes, but I maturely ignored her challenge.

"Do you or do you not recall which of the brothers-in-law was the object of Rebecca's attention?" I asked.

"Rudy Gerber. But I'm sure the other men got their share of attention too. Rebecca Miller was a wanton woman."

"Why, Freni, how you talk!"

"It's true, Magdalena. Her parents should have named her Rahab, after that harlot in the Bible."

I was shocked. Freni is a one-woman Supreme Court, but words like "wanton" and "harlot" don't come easily to her lips. Rebecca Miller Weaver must have led a wild life, even by today's standards.

"Freni, you implied earlier that the whole Miller bunch was strange. What exactly did you mean?"

"You've seen them," she practically shrieked. "Calling themselves the Beeftrust. Imagine that!"

"Being tall and big-boned is no sin, dear," I reminded her charitably. Freni, who is only a smidgen over five feet tall, harbors a deep resentment of anyone who can cast a shadow after ten in the morning.

"But they all married shorter men, Magdalena. The Bible warns us not to get unequally yoked. You know, like hooking oxen together with asses."

I smiled patiently. If you let her, Freni would prove that the pope is Jewish.

"The Bible is talking about spiritual equals, not physical. Just because they call themselves the Beeftrust doesn't mean they're oxen."

Freni's stuck her lower lip out so far that had she been in a rainstorm she would have drowned. I knew she was thinking hard, sorting through almost seventy-five years of memories for proof that the Millers really were a weird bunch. Her eyes brightened suddenly.

"They all moved out of Hernia, didn't they?" she crowed triumphantly.

"And that makes them strange?"

"Well, even you haven't moved away from Hernia!"

I turned my head so she wouldn't see me stick my tongue out. "Try again, dear. If remaining in Hernia is a sign of relative normality, then your daughter- in-law, Barbara, is supernormal. After all, she moved from somewhere else to here."

"Ach du lieber!" Freni clearly saw the logic in what I had said. It was the same sort of logic that had her convinced that eggs were a fruit.

"Well?"

She stared at me, beaten but far from broken. "Well, I wasn't going to bring this up, but now you've forced me to. Right, Magdalena?"

"You're absolutely right, dear. Consider yourself forced."

She sighed in relief. "In that case, you should know that in the autumn the Miller family held a private memorial service."

"Why, of course! They had every reason to suspect that something terrible had happened to Sarah. And it had."

"Yah, but from what I heard, the service was for both mother and daughter. Imagine that, and the mother up in the Poconos having a good time."

"You don't know that, Freni. Has anyone ever heard from Rebecca since then?"

"Not a peep."

"And her husband, Jonas? What happened to him?"

She shrugged. "The police questioned him. Several times even, but they let him go. I think I heard once that he lives in Florida now."

I would have pressed her for even more details of that fateful summer, but Leah had awakened from her nap and, smelling food, had homed straight in on the kitchen.

The two older women got immediately embroiled in a polite but heavy conversation on the right way to make a tongue sandwich. Actually, they may have quarreled, but with the two of them it's hard to tell. At any rate, while they were thus engaged, I took my tongue and got out of there.

7

It was another perfect day. Lying as it does in a mountain valley, Hernia tends toward cloudy weather. Not so this Saturday afternoon. There weren't even enough wisps to wind around one cotton candy stick. The temperature was perfect too—somewhere in the mid-seventies.

I took the same path I had taken on that fateful day when I fell in love with my Pooky Bear. The path led out of my driveway, across Hertzler Lane, and over a split rail fence. From there it wound through a lush green pasture—carefully avoiding the cow pies—to the banks of Miller's Pond. This day, however, I extended the path to the far side of the pasture and into the Miller family farmyard.

Since Aaron and his dad were out shopping, there was no one around except for the cows, an assortment of barn cats, and two or three million sparrows. It was both peaceful and noisy.

I sat on Aaron's front steps for a few minutes, imagining what it would have been like to be mistress of that domain. It would never be, of course. Aaron and I had decided that we would make the PennDutch our home, although he would continue to give his father a hand with the farm. Eventually the farm would be sold and Aaron would devote his time to helping me run the inn. This was not my idea, mind you. Aaron is not buggy-whipped, no matter what you're thinking.

While I was sitting there, a large female cat, misnamed Cyrus, jumped into my lap and began twitching her tail nastily in my face. I pushed her off, but she jumped right back up. Before I could push her off again, she started yowling seductively, kneading my thighs with her front paws. Immediately three male cats jumped onto the porch and approached Cyrus and me with great enthusiasm. It was all too horrible for words.

"Get off, Rahab!" I shouted, standing up.

But Cyrus didn't seem to mind being called a harlot, and she didn't get off. She had dug her nails into my denim skirt and, whether she intended to do so or not, had become part of my apparel. Unless you've tried, you have no idea how hard it is to dislodge a cat's claws from fabric. I tried mightily, but it was no use.

There was only one option that I could think of, and that was the garden hose (taking off my skirt and walking home in my Hanes Her Way was never an option). Cyrus was heavy, and I staggered off the porch trailed by three horny, howling toms. Had Aaron or his father been home to see the strange procession, I'm sure there never would have been a wedding.

Fortunately the water did the trick, and Cyrus departed my denim, but not without first inflicting some nasty scratches—narrowly missing places my mama didn't have names for. Needless to say, I had to get drenched in the process, and while the temperature may have been perfect for walking, it wasn't too pleasant for water activities. Therefore I will claim distraction as a valid excuse when I confess that out of the corner of my left eye I saw something bigger than a cat dart toward the barn, but I could not identify it. Whatever it was, it wasn't a cow. Cows don't dart.

I trotted over to the barn, which was open, and peered inside. Approximately half of the floor space was empty save for a rather thick layer of loose hay and dust. Mama would have called it "strubbly," the Amish word for messy. On the other side of the barn, a jumble of hay bales extended almost halfway up to the rafters. On top of the bales a dozen cats lounged. They regarded me indolently.

"Okay, so I'm imagining things," I said aloud. "I'm losing my marbles with only a week left before my wedding."

Behind me I heard a low, jarring thump. I whirled around, but nobody was there. I may as well confess that I screamed nonetheless. The echo of my voice in the half-empty barn gave me the heebie-jeebies, and I fled out into the warm sunshine.

I am not a superstitious person, mind you, but I do believe in ghosts. I know, good Mennonites eschew such beliefs, but I guess my devotion to my faith will just have to remain suspect. I believe in ghosts because I have seen one. The specter I saw was my Grandma Yoder, and no one—not even my pastor—can tell me I didn't. And I didn't see Grandma just out of the corner of my eye either. I saw her, clear as day, in the bed in which she died— a week after she was buried. So real was Grandma that had I sat on the bed next to her, she would have snapped at me for messing up the covers.

Maybe it's because I live in a predominantly cloudy climate, but I think sunshine can heal just about anything. As my skirt dried, my cowardice vanished, and within twenty minutes I was ready for anything—except another close encounter with Cyrus. It was in this moment of sun-charged energy that I forgot my limitations and recklessly set out to investigate the

Miller family root cellar. It was from there that the barrel of kraut containing Sarah Weaver had come.

This root cellar is a subterranean room with stone walls and heavy wooden doors that open upward and outward. It adjoins the foundation of the house, on the north side, and there is a narrow door that leads from it into the basement proper. Aaron says that visitors from the Midwest have compared the cellar to a tornado shelter. Having never been to the Midwest, I wouldn't know. I can only hope Midwestern children have as much fun playing in their storm cellars as Aaron and I did in his root cellar (when we were kids, I mean).

If I remembered correctly, the Millers kept a padlock in the door hasp, but they never locked it. Aaron said there was no need to, since the back door of the house was never locked anyway. The padlock, like the sometimes locked front door, was just for show. Now, however, the lock was gone altogether, no doubt in the possession of the maniac mantis, Melvin.

I tugged on one of the heavy doors. It seemed stuck at first, and then it fairly flew into my face, knocking me over backward. It was just as well that I was sitting down, because I would have sat down just as hard when I saw that face grinning up at me.

The face belonged to Uncle Elias Fike, Auntie Magdalena's husband. "Whoa! Didn't mean for that to happen!" it said.

I struggled for several minutes to catch my breath. My speaking voice came back a few seconds after that. I will edit those first words out of my mouth, on the chance that some of you still have standards. I must admit—and shamefully so—that mine had been gradually slipping, thanks to Susannah. She knows foul words for things Mama didn't even know existed.

"Hey, I said I was sorry," Elias repeated. "You gave me a quite a start as well. What are you doing here?"

"Me? I'm not the one caught snooping in someone else's cellar, am I?"

He had the nerve to smile. "No? Then why are we having this conversation?"

"Beats me. I'm not actually in the cellar, am I?"

"Well, I'm a member of the family, so I have a right to be here."

"You're only connected by marriage, which is exactly what I'll be too, come next Saturday. So don't think you're one up in the rights department."

He bowed slightly. "In that case, by all means come on down. But there's nothing down here worth seeing."

"Says who?"

"Look for yourself."

"What's in those barrels?"

"Sauerkraut, cider, and pickles. Of course, now it will spoil because someone has pried open the tops."

"Melvin."

"I beg your pardon?"

"Our local constable." Would that he were. The worst English constable would have it hands down over Melvin when it came to brains. Or personality, for that matter. No, if Melvin were British, he'd be a member of the royal family.

"You never did say what you are doing here. Don't you have a root cellar of your own?"

"My mother was color-blind," I said.

"What?"

It was a trick I learned from Susannah. When cornered, divert the enemy's attention and then sneak away. So to speak.

"I said my mother was color-blind."

"I heard what you said. What's it supposed to mean?"

He had confused me, possibly a diversionary plan of his own. "It means what it means. She was, and I'm not."

"Are you saying your mother wasn't a racist, but you are?"

"What?"

"Because if it bothers you to marry into a family with an African American member, maybe you should think again. I've been married to Magdalena for fifty-two years, and I don't plan to get a divorce anytime soon."

I stared openmouthed long enough to collect a snootful of flies before the cerebral lightning hit. Fortunately there was a light breeze, which kept insects at bay.

"I meant color blindness literally. My mama couldn't tell blue from purple, or green from brown. It's a very rare condition in women, you know, but it does happen. Since Mama almost always wore navy or black, it didn't matter much in clothes, but I used to have to help her choose her embroidery thread."

"So?"

"So, your left sock is brown, your right sock is green."

He had a deep, hearty laugh. "Yeah, well, if my wife would sort them, it wouldn't happen so much."

"You could learn to sort them yourself. She could mark the pair with letters or numbers and then you could sort them when you took them out of the dryer. You do your own laundry, don't you?"

"Poor Aaron," he muttered, shaking his head.

"What?"

He sprinted up the stone steps, which surprised me. "I said, 'Poor Aaron.' It's not going to be fun hauling all those barrels up here just to throw it all away."

I looked him over closely. "You're pretty fast on your feet, you know."

"You mean, for a man my age, don't you?" He laughed.

"Were you in the barn earlier?"

"Earlier when? I've been in that barn lots of times. I'm already family, remember?"

I swallowed my irritation, since it had no calories. "Earlier this afternoon. Like just a few minutes ago."

"No. No offense, but I got bored hanging around at your place and wandered on over here. Decided to check out the root cellar—call it morbid curiosity if you will—but I had no reason to mess with the barn. Why? Is something wrong with it?"

"Very funny. Do you mind telling me why you had the cellar doors closed when you were in it? Or is this something I don't want to know?"

"You're a gas, Miss Yoder, you know that?"

"You may call me Ethel, then," I said drily.

"Ha, ha. Well, if you must know, I didn't close the doors. They fell. Nearly hit me on the head. I could have been the second corpse carried up these stairs."

That certainly explained the thump I'd heard when I was in the barn. As for the darter—well, I would have to keep that appointment with my optometrist this year. When you have to hold the hymnbook further away than your arm can reach, your body is telling you something.

I made a dignified retreat and retraced my steps across the pasture. At least I thought I had.

"Ach, du heimer," Freni gasped when I walked in the back door. "What is that smell?"

I glanced down to see that one of my steps had been ill-placed.

8

"How did lunch go over?" I asked Freni.

"Ach, that Leah! Just like a Troyer to want mustard on a tongue sandwich."

"She was born a Miller," I reminded her. "And what's wrong with mustard?"

"On fruit?" she asked incredulously.

I fled the kitchen before she could tell me her rationale.

Three of the aunties were still in the dining room. However, they weren't eating—they were quilting. I keep a quilt-in-progress stretched out on a frame in one corner of the room and allow my guests to try their hand at the craft. Actually, I encourage them to do so. Amish and Mennonite quilts, even poorly made ones, are very popular with tourists. As long as machines rule the world, "handmade" items will continue to fetch a premium.

"Everything all right?" I asked graciously.

Auntie Veronica's nose rose and twitched a few times.

"You tell us," Auntie Leah boomed.

"I left my shoes on the back porch," I said quickly. "And that's not what I was talking about."

I caught Veronica stealing a glance at her own tiny tootsies. "Well, if you were asking about our rooms," she said, "I'd have to say no."

"Sorry, dear, but you're not getting mine. We've already been over that," I said for the benefit of the other two.

"You see what I mean?" she said to her sisters. She turned to me. "There has been no maid service yet today, Magdalena. Are you going to make poor little Aaron change my sheets again?"

I smiled patiently. "Of course not, dear. For the next week we're all on the ALPO plan. You get to do your own room. And cheer up. Usually I charge extra for that, but on account of you're family, this time I won't."

Veronica did not beam with gratitude. "I would have stayed in a hotel, you know, but Van Doren's Guide to Gracious Living doesn't list a five-star establishment for Bedford County."

"Well!" I said. What else could I say? Robert Van Doren had not been amused by the ALPO plan, and when I shut off the hot water in the middle of one of his twenty-minute showers, he was possibly even irritated.

"I would have stayed in any hotel," Leah barked, "except that the Bottomless Pit has drained me dry again."

"The Bottomless Pit?" I asked politely.

Six pairs of eyes narrowed. "Family business," Veronica hissed.

I started to leave.

"Kissed a bitch," my namesake whimpered.

I ran that through my brain until it came out "missed a stitch." Then I generously showed her how to rectify the problem, complimented them all, and set off in search of Auntie Lizzie, the sane one.

She wasn't in the parlor, but all four uncles were. They were sprawled out and snoring like overslopped hogs—except that hogs don't wear suits and ties eighteen hours a day. It surprised me to see Elias among them. I hadn't dawdled much on the way home, and the pasture route is a lot shorter than using the lane. Still, he appeared not only to have beaten me back but to have fallen into a deep sleep as well. No doubt it had something to do with the water back in St. Louis.

I silently retraced my steps, and was just reaching for the doorknob when I felt something brush against my skirt. Actually—and it pains me to say this—it felt like something pinched me on my left buttock. I glanced behind me, and while it may have been only my imagination, it appeared to me that Uncle Rudy's left arm was not where it had been a moment before. He, however, was still snoring as loudly, if not louder, than the others.

"Do that again, buster, and you'll have to use your toes to help you count," I whispered. I maintain that I am a nonviolent person, and when I closed the parlor door behind me, I put that ugly scene right out of my mind.

I found Lizzie on the front porch, in one of the white wicker rockers I put out seasonally. She had commandeered a little wicker table and was doing her nails. Frankly, I was shocked. She was the very first Mennonite I'd seen to be thus engaged. Susannah, who barely qualifies as a lapsed Presbyterian, doesn't count.

I would have told Lizzie that nail polish drew unwanted attention to her huge hands, but she seemed glad for my company, so I curbed my tongue.

"Who or what is the Bottomless Pit?" I asked pleasantly.

Her eyes narrowed as well. "Family business, dear."

"Well, I am practically family, aren't I?"

"Yes, as a matter of fact you are. But you really don't want to know any sooner than you have to. Trust me."

I nodded. I would simply ask Freni. She would know. I could afford to switch the subject.

"Nice out here today, isn't it?"

"I love this place," she agreed enthusiastically.

"Thank you. I'm rather fond of it myself."

"Of course! No, what I meant was I love Hernia. It's so peaceful here."

"Hernia? Is Du Bois a big city?"

She had a cultivated laugh, the kind you would expect from a woman with platinum hair. "Compared to Hernia, it is. God, I miss it here."

I was both stunned and thrilled. I had never known a Mennonite woman—one still active in her church—who used the name of our creator casually like that in a sentence. I didn't approve, mind you, but it excited me to think that there was another way of looking at things besides my own, and besides that of those folks who were obviously headed for hell in a hand basket. Like the Presbyterians and the Methodists.

"I've always wanted to travel," I said wistfully. "This year I got to go to Farmersburg, Ohio, but that's it. And I've never lived anyplace else."

"Count your blessings."

That was easy for her to say. She was polishing the nails on her right hand, and her left hand wasn't even trembling. Clearly, she felt no wrong. Heaven and nail polish too! One couldn't get any more blessed than that.

"If you like it here so much, why did you leave? Was it Uncle Manasses's job?"

She gave me a queer look. "His job?"

"Just guessing."

"You guessed right. Manny was a tobacco salesman. He used to travel all the time, so we could have made his base of operations anywhere. But you know how folks around here are."

"Yup. Susannah claims that Hernia is the buckle on the Bible belt. Our cousin Sam, who owns the only food market, was picketed when he added wine vinegar to his stock."

She laughed till she shook. "Oh, shit," she said. "See what you made me do?"

Hopefully I hadn't caused her to swear. Nails, I supposed, could be fixed, but Mama spinning in her coffin was a grave matter.

"Auntie Lizzie, could I ask you some personal questions?"

"Lizzie, please. And there's no need to ask. That isn't Manny's real hair color. Or the color of his mustache either. When I started coloring my hair—I do, you know—Manny had to follow suit. He thought if I was going to look young, then he had to as well. Like I would step out on him!"

That wasn't what I was going to ask, but I decided to run with it. "Forgive me if this is a painful subject, but did your sister Rebecca really run off to the Poconos with an accordion-playing preacher?"

She knocked the polish bottle over, but an oversized hand righted it again before any damage was done.

"Who told you that?"

"Heard it around," I said. As much as Freni irritates me, I would rather put bamboo slivers under my fingernails than betray her. I'd even rather eat fried liver and mashed turnips, which says a lot.

"Well, there was an accordion player, but she sure as hell didn't run off with him."

"Again, I don't mean to be rude, but how can you be so sure?"

She took her time before answering, blowing on each magnificent finger like it was a candle with a stubborn wick.

"Because, dear, it was Vonnie who had the affair with Benjamin, not Becca."

I gulped. "Auntie Veronica?"

"Well, I can't actually prove that they had an affair affair, if you know what I mean."

I nodded, although it was machts-nichts to me. What did I know about the various levels of an affair? It didn't matter, though, because Lizzie loved to talk.

"It was a terrible idea in the first place, that twenty-fifth wedding anniversary party. Aaron Senior and Catherine were never happily married. So why celebrate twenty-five years of bickering?"

"Why, indeed?"

"Because that's what our family does. So we all dropped everything and made happy for a week. Fortunately none of us lived out of state, so it wasn't a big financial hardship, except maybe for Vonnie and Rudy. You'd think Verona was on the moon, the way she complained."

"I thought they lived in Fox Chapel."

She had a cultivated chuckle. "They do now, of course, but back then they didn't have enough change to play tiddle-dywinks."

"I've been to Verona," I felt compelled to say. "It's right next to Oakmont, where Mystery Lovers Bookshop is located. Fox Chapel is on the other side of the Allegheny River."

"Exactly. Well, Vonnie bitched for about a day or two, and then she saw this sign for a revival, and the next thing we knew, she had fallen head over heels in love with the accordion player."

"Was he cute?"

Platinum blondes don't always emit cultivated laughs. "He was as ugly as a mangy hound dog dead two days."

"That bad?"

"Honey, none of us could see what she saw in him. Of course, Rudy may not be so much to look at now, but in those days he was a hell of a lot cuter than that accordion player."

"Maybe she was having trouble with her marriage," I said meekly. The meekness part was important. Most married folks bristle when a spinster offers an opinion on the subject.

"Yeah, well, that's a whole book in itself."

"Do tell. The high points, I mean."

"You sure this won't offend your sensibilities?"

"Positive." At least not any more than the question itself had.

"Rudy Gerber considers himself God's gift to women."

"I noticed."

"He put the squeeze on you?"

"I felt like I was an orange."

"Welcome to the club. Unfortunately that's not as bad as it gets."

"So he had affair affairs?"

She looked me over casually, like I was a horse she was about to bid on. "Of course I can't prove that he did, but everyone knows he did. Especially after they moved to Verona. From what I hear, that place is a real fleshpot."

I felt cheated for having noticed nothing more than a quaint riverside town whose main street was lined with antique shops.

"And Rudy is a Mennonite?"

"Born and bred." The cultivated laugh returned. "Honey, Mennonites are just like everyone else."

Not the ones I knew. Not in Hernia. I grew up thinking we had it all over the Catholic church. They had just one Virgin Mary with a son; we had hundreds.

"So you think Veronica ran around with the accordion player to get back at Rudy?"

"Two and two makes four, doesn't it?"

I sat quietly for a few minutes watching her paint the enormous nails on her gargantuan hands. If I had nails that big, and the courage to paint them, I would feel compelled to paint scenes from the Gospels. One of her thumbnails alone could hold the Feeding of the Five Thousand—if done with a very small brush, of course.

"About Rebecca," I said at last, "a little bird told me that Rudy was pestering her that summer. You know what I mean. And that it made Jonas, Rebecca's husband, jealous. Is that true?"

"Does this little bird put mint jelly on tongue sandwiches?"

"Let's say it's possible."

"Ah, Freni, of course. I know she's your auntie, but—"

"My mother's cousin, actually."

"She doesn't always get things right."

I nodded to encourage her, but I felt terribly guilty. One woman I liked but hardly knew. The other I loved (you try liking Freni!).

"Rudy may have been pursuing Becca, but Jonas was not the least bit bothered by it. He trusted Becca completely. No, I'd say he was more flattered by Rudy's attention than bothered."

"I'll set her straight." And I would. Mustard versus mint jelly on tongue was a no-brainer, as Susannah was fond of saying.

I spent far too much time watching Lizzie paint her nails, and when I was absolutely sure that none of them were going to sport biblical scenes, I decided to sneak back to my room—past the log-sawing uncles—and take a brief nap of my own. Stress, I have discovered, can manifest itself two ways. Either it makes you feel like swinging from the barn rafters, screeching at the top of your lungs, or it knocks you into a near coma. At that moment I could hardly keep my eyes open.

I screamed.

"Damn it!" the body said and sat up.

"Susannah!" I lunged at the light.

Sure enough, there was my baby sister, swaddled in her silken swirls, but something was clearly amiss. It took me several seconds to realize that she was crying. Tears are not something I am used to seeing on Susannah's cheeks.

"Susannah, whatever is the matter?"

I patted her arm out of the deepest concern. I suppose you will take me to task for not hugging her, but I am genetically incapable of such behavior unless the recipient is less than two feet tall.

"It's you," she said accusingly and flopped back down.

"What?"

"You're the trouble."

"Susannah, I had no idea when I accepted the kraut—"

"I'm not talking about the damn kraut, Mags. I'm talking about your wedding."

"Susannah, I've made you my bridesmaid. What else do you want?"

I already knew the answer to that. She had made it painfully clear. My sister wanted her dress to be hot pink and cut well above the knee. The only reason she wasn't pushing for a low-cut model was that she had plans to carry Shnookums in her bra up the aisle!

"Oh, Mags, it's so unfair."

I took a deep breath and counted to ten—by fives. "I will not have a dog at my wedding, dear. You can cry until your eyes fall out, but I'm not changing my mind. Do you think there was a canine at the wedding in Cana?"

"You are so dense sometimes," she wailed and rolled over on the bed. There was a stifled yelp and she hastily sat up.

"Then illuminate me, dear."

"I'm not talking about Shnookums. I'm talking about you—and marriage."

"What?"

"I never thought I would see you get married, Mags."

"Thanks a lot."

"No, I mean I'm not sure I'm ready for it."

"Go on."

"This is hard, Mags."

"Go on anyway." To make it as easy as I could, I turned slightly away. I, for one, have always found talking to a face intimidating.

"Well—remember how it was when Mama and Papa died? I don't mean that day, exactly, but afterward."

These were rhetorical questions, and I understood them fully. From the moment I saw the state trooper's car in the drive, I felt like I was sleepwalking. That feeling persisted for days. And then when the numbness wore off, I felt panic. Grief didn't catch up until much later.

I nodded.

"Well, that's how I feel now."

"Numb, or panicky?"

"Panicky. I'm scared to death, Mags."

"Of what?"

"Of what will happen to me."

"What on earth do you mean?"

"Will you make me leave, Mags?"

"Leave? The PennDutch?"

"Ever since that day, Mags, it's been us sisters alone against the world. Just us and Shnookums. The Three Musketeers."

"Your rat would be a mouseketeer," I said, not unkindly.

"You get my point, Mags. We've always had each other."

Except for your ill-fated marriage, when you just ran off and left me, I felt like saying, but I didn't.

"Of course I don't expect you to leave," I said, after a brief and perhaps evil pause.

"You don't?"

"Not on your life! I'm going to need you even more when I'm married."

"You will?"

"You bet your sweet bippy. When I'm a married woman, I'm going to want some time off—if you know what I mean—and I expect you to take up the slack."

"What kind of slack?"

"Well, for starters, there are those folks who are too cheap for ALPO. You'll—"

"You want me to do laundry and clean rooms?"

"Bingo! And Freni could use a hand in the kitchen from time to time. She's no spring chicken, you know."

"Enough! I feel needed," Susannah wailed. It was a happy wail, though, and Shnookums felt free to join in. Over the years they have learned to harmonize.

"But the pooch stays home from church," I said sternly. "I'm nervous enough without having to worry about doggy-doo when I'm saying my I do's."

"Speaking of nervous—are you, Mags?"

"I just said I was, dear."

"I mean, about sex."

"What?"

"It will be your first time, won't it?"

I stared at my sister. I couldn't believe that even she would ask me such a thing. In my book, it was unnecessary. The asking, not the sex—although I wasn't convinced about that either. I was most definitely still a virgin. And of course I wasn't nervous— I was petrified!

Mama (and in his own clumsy way, Papa) raised me to believe that sex before marriage was wrong. I'm not saying that I had a lot of opportunity to disappoint them, but as long as one heterosexual male roams the earth, there isn't a woman alive that needs to die a virgin. But I had been a good girl and saved myself for marriage. I only hoped I hadn't waited too long.

Dr. Carr (a woman) in Bedford had informed me that everything was in working order. Not necessarily prime, mind you, but working. She had assured me that Aaron, if he was half the man I claimed he was, would take things slowly until the machinery was raring to go. She even had some exercises I might do, to "facilitate the transition." But as kind and helpful as Dr. Carr was, she hadn't managed to vanquish all my fears.

"I'm terrified," I wailed.

"There, there," Susannah said, and against all genetic opposition, she hugged me close.

We had never felt more like sisters.

9

The Beeftrust and their respective consorts filled an entire pew the next morning at Beechy Grove Mennonite Church. Aaron, his dad, and I sat behind them. Freni and her husband, Mose, went to their Amish services, and Susannah just stayed home. I don't think even the Presbyterians have seen her in a month of Sundays.

Rev. Michael Schrock is a very young man—just two years out of seminary—and Hernia is his first pastorate. His wife, Lodema, is our new organist. They have no children. It is my impression that everyone is fond of the couple, but if truth be told, most of us wish that Rev. Schrock would preach shorter sermons and that Lodema would play the hymns as they appear in the book. Her embellishments, while quite creative, do not enhance the service. There, I said it—and said it like a good Christian, I might add.

The Beeftrust, however, enjoyed themselves thoroughly. They sang loudly—and off-key—trailing along behind Lodema's strange departures, oblivious to pace or place. During the sermon three of them pulled yarn out of their purses and began knitting away, as busy as bees constructing a hive.

Because of their size, no one saw them—except the choir and of course the Schrocks. Frankly, I wouldn't have known what they were up to but for the faint click of needles and the skein of lavender yarn that somehow escaped and came to a stop at my feet.

The uncles took advantage of the forty-five-minute dissertation on the joys of tithing to supplement their nap time. Being good Mennonite uncles, they knew, to a man, how to church-sleep. I had always believed this to be an inherited ability, so I was pleased to see that Uncle Elias was just as adept at it as the others. Their heads bobbed only occasionally, never inclining to more than a sixty-degree angle. Their snores were as soft as a kitten's.

After church we dillydallied in the parking lot while my soon-to-be-in-laws gave thumbnail autobiographies of themselves to old friends and received tome-length accounts of their friends' lives in return. "Fine," "great," and "never been better" were the lies most often voiced by visitors and regulars alike.

For some reason I got chosen as Lodema's sounding board that morning. Apparently the choir was suffering from spring fever, the organ needed major repairs, and the prices at Sam Yoder's Comer Market were far too high. Then she got around to her real agenda. Did I realize her husband was under a lot of strain, she wondered? I did not. Was I aware that the following weekend was the Annual Trout Fishing Championship in Scaleybark, West Virginia? I was not. Under the circumstances, would I consider postponing my wedding so Michael could unwind over his favorite flies? I most certainly would not! I said it as politely as I could, but Lodema still ended up in tears.

By the time I was ready to leave, everyone but Aaron and his dad—and of course the Schrocks— had long since departed. Even the Beeftrust had taken hoof, although surely they knew that Sunday dinner would not be served until I got there.

I would like to state here that if Aaron hadn't been so impatient to get home he might have noticed in time that the left rear tire on the car—my car—was a little low. But he didn't notice until the loud frump, frump, frump of a total flat punctured the relative silence of the peaceful countryside. By then we were halfway home.

"Damn!" Aaron said and got out to extract the spare.

Worse words, army words, surfaced when he discovered I was packing no spare.

"It's Susannah's fault," I wailed. "She borrowed it last week to go into Bedford. She must have had a flat then and not told me. How was I to know she didn't replace the spare?"

Aaron said a few choice phrases that made me think, albeit temporarily, that it might well be in our best interests to postpone the wedding. Maybe a weekend of fly-fishing in West Virginia would straighten out some of the kinks that were rapidly showing up in his armor.

In the end my Pooky Bear left me to keep his dad company while he strode the five or so miles home to get his car. Although there were several farms along the way, they were owned by Amish families, who possessed neither spare tires nor telephones. It was also unlikely that he would get a lift. At that hour everyone else was long home from church and if not deeply immersed in their Sunday dinners, already beginning to sleep them off.

"Mr. Miller—"

"Pops, please," said Aaron's octogenarian father. "That's what my son calls me. You do the same. After all, you are going to be my daughter come Saturday."

"Okay, Pops." It had a certain spring to it. "Anyway, sorry about this flat business."

He smiled, and I'm sure his mouth had to work hard to push aside the wrinkles. "I'm not. I wanted a chance to talk to you alone."

"You did? Look, Pops, I'm not marrying your son for your money. I inherited my own farm, and thanks to the PennDutch, I have all the money I'll ever need."

I was charmed by his laugh, although it did sound like a frog croaking. "I always knew you had a good head on your shoulders, Magdalena. Not like what's-her-name."

"Her name is Susannah," I said loyally, "and she's been your neighbor for thirty-four years, ever since the day she was born."

"Ah, yes, Susannah. At my age, names and dates sometimes get lost. Anyway, I'm glad to hear that you are financially set, because Aaron isn't going to inherit anything."

"What?" I didn't mean to say it so loud.

"My father took a big loss in the Depression, and we inherited a huge mortgage. Then back in the seventies we had to remortgage the place—soaring fuel prices for the machinery and falling beef prices. Something about steak being high in cholesterol. At any rate, I'm broke."

"You're kidding."

"No, no, I'm sure it's true. Beefworld had an article on cholesterol—"

"I mean about being broke, dear."

His shoulders, already sagging under the weight of eighty years, sagged further. "I don't make jokes about money, Magdalena. If I sold the farm tomorrow and paid off all my debts, I would still owe money."

"How much?"

"Maybe a couple of thousand."

"I could loan you that," I said charitably. I tithe from my income, and it could just as well go straight to Aaron Senior instead of taking a bypass through the offering plate. That being the case, I wouldn't even ask for the money back.

He smiled, revealing teeth that were obviously his. "Thank you. That's very kind. But you wouldn't tell Aaron about it, would you?"

"He doesn't know?"

"I'm sure he suspects, but he doesn't know the details. Not unless one of the others told him."

"The others?"

"My sisters."

"The Beeftrust?" I clamped my hand over my mouth, but it was too late. Words can't be stuffed back in like cookie crumbs.

He chuckled. "Why do you think they call themselves that? It's not their size, you know. It's because they're co-owners of my farm."

"What?"

He nodded. "The farm was left jointly to all of us. I would have bought them out, but like I said, I didn't have two nickels to rub together at the time."

"You still don't," I said gently.

"My sisters didn't want to sell anyway. They'd all grown up on the farm and liked the idea of owning a piece of it. They also liked the idea of running things, even if they didn't like the work."

"Tell me about it, Pops. Susannah wants me to turn the PennDutch into a retirement home for movie stars. Golly-wood, she wants to call it. But she can't even take out the trash without being told three times."

"My sisters—well, you've seen them—could have each done a man's job. We could have turned the farm into the biggest cattle spread east of the Mississippi if they had done more than just talk about what they wanted."

Our eyes met in sibling-inspired sympathy. Sisters! There when you don't need them, gone when you do.

"But cheer up," I said brightly, "from now on things are going to be looking up."

"No, they won't."

"How do you mean?"

"The money I owe is to my sisters."

"You are the Bottomless Pit?"

"The farm, Magdalena, not me. You can't run a farm with a bunch of bosses and just one working hand. Even the Bible will tell you that."

"They all have different ideas?"

"They and their husbands. No two of us could ever agree on anything. I thought we should stick with Aberdeen Angus, but Lizzie thought Shorthorns were more practical. Leah wanted Herefords, but oh, no, Vonnie just had to have Charolais. They were so pretty, she said. As for Magdalena—"

"So you went in every direction but up?" Some folks need a little help in summarizing.

"Yes. And guess who gets the blame?"

"Well, they'll get over it as soon as you sell the farm and pay them back."

"And then what?"

"And then you'll finally have some peace."

He stared at me. His eyes had once been an intense blue like his son's, but they were faded now, like bleached denim. And the irises were crosshatched, like denim, with tiny lines.

"Won't you?" I asked.

"But where?"

I waved a hand. "Wherever you decide to go. Florida, maybe. Or the Mennonite Home for the Aged over in Somerset."

His throat laughed, but his eyes didn't. "Just like I thought. You don't really understand, Magdalena. I am broke—or I will be as soon as I get out of debt. Farmers don't have pensions."

I stared back. I felt like I had that time, after Susannah's divorce, when she stopped by the inn on a pretense of borrowing a vacuum cleaner. I should have bolted the doors and piled heavy furniture in front of the windows. I should have had my mail held and my phone disconnected. I should have remained in seclusion, until somebody—perhaps God Himself—sent a white dove down the chimney with a note attached telling me that Susannah was now a safe six states away, married, and the mother of five children.

Imagine! Susannah Yoder Entwhistle wanting to borrow a vacuum cleaner! Imagine Aaron Miller Sr., a man of fewer words than Michelangelo's David, pouring out his troubles to me. And broke? Mennonites may be poor, but they are too frugal ever to be broke. Or so I had thought. Yesiree, if I had had half the sense of a heifer, I would have hoofed it out of there right then. I would have galloped right past Aaron, thrown everyone out of the inn, and barricaded the windows and doors just like I should have done with Susannah.

"Just what is your point, dear?" I asked kindly.

Aaron Senior swallowed hard, his Adam's apple bobbing like a tied cork with a big bass on the other end.

"I'm asking you and Aaron to take me in, Magdalena."

I'm sure my Eve's apple bobbed a few times at that point. "Me? Us?"

"Yes."

"But what about your sisters?"

"They wouldn't have me. Far too much resentment. On all our parts," he added with admirable honesty.

"Your nephews and nieces?" I asked. Hope does indeed spring eternal—especially when in-laws are involved.

He shrugged. "I've never been close to any of them. Besides, Aaron is my son. Folks would expect him to take me in first."

To his credit, Aaron Senior stopped just short of saying that it was his son's duty. It might not seem like that to you now, but believe me, there is a world of difference between performing an act of generosity and an act of duty. The former might possibly stir up feelings of noble pride in one's breast, the latter only resentment. Again, I am talking about in-laws.

The rock and the hard place waited patiently for me to answer while I gasped, snorted, cleared my throat, and repeated the combination in every possible sequence. Eighty years had given him a different perception of time.

"Well," I said at last, "Aaron and I would be delighted to have you come and live with us."

"You would?"

I broke the ninth commandment twice in a row.

I'm not saying the blue returned to his eyes or his shoulders stopped sagging, but Aaron Senior suddenly seemed years younger.

"I wouldn't be any trouble, honest. And I promise not to give you unsolicited advice about your marriage."

"And think twice about solicited advice," I warned him. "I've been known to kill the messenger—so to speak."

"I understand."

I took a deep breath. "But of course it will cost you."

"I beg your pardon?"

"What I mean is, I need something from you in return for free room and board for the rest of your life."

The poor man blushed deeply.

"Why, Pops Miller, watch what you think! I'm talking about some information."

He sighed. "Freni told me you'd ask. The truth is, Aaron really is two years younger than you."

I waved a hand impatiently. "I don't care about that," I said, breaking that same commandment yet a third time. "I want to know what really went on between your sisters and that accordion-playing evangelist, Benjamin Somebody-or-another."

"Ah, that. It's important, is it?"

"If you want a roof over your head, it is," I said. I didn't mean to be insensitive, it just slipped out. "You see, I don't feel right marrying your son until we've had a funeral for your niece, and—"

"Rebecca did not run off to the Poconos with that two-bit, small-tent evangelist," he said emphatically. "I know that's probably one of the versions you've heard, but it isn't true."

"How can you be so positive? I mean, no one ever heard from her again."

Like many men of his generation, Aaron Senior prefers to wear suspenders. He hooked two claw-like thumbs under them and pulled hard. One slipped digit and his tummy would be in for quite a smack.

"I just know."

"Yes, but Freni says she did. Lizzie, however—"

"I'm positive because it was my Catherine who ran off with the accordion player."

My mouth opened and closed like a hungry baby bird. Fortunately I was given the grace not to put my foot into it.

"I see. I'm so sorry."

"Don't be. She came back the very next day—apparently that preacher fellow couldn't practice what he preached. If you get my drift."

I did, and nodded. I am not as naive as Susannah thinks I am.

"But by then Rebecca had disappeared. Of course everyone thought that it was she who ran off with the guy. I only wish she had. She might still be alive!"

He choked back a sob. I waited until he motioned me to continue.

"Pops, why didn't you tell people what really happened?"

"Because of my son. Catherine begged me not to tell anyone about her 'mistake.' She said it would destroy Aaron."

"Kids are tougher than you think," I said stupidly. "Besides, Aaron was already a young man then."

"I know. Hindsight is always perfect, isn't it? In the end our nasty little secret destroyed both Catherine and Rebecca, but not Aaron."

"He knows?"

He looked startled. "No, of course not."

"I'd tell him if I were you. He's bound to find out someday."

"You?"

"No, not me. The truth always has a way of coming out—eventually. But tell me what you meant about Catherine and Rebecca both being destroyed by the secret."

"Yes, that. Rebecca was the first victim." Even after twenty years I could hear the pain in his voice. "If we hadn't been trying to protect my wife's reputation, we could have stopped the rumors that it was Rebecca who ran off with the preacher. Then the police would have taken her disappearance more seriously. They might have found her before it was too late. As for Catherine, she wasn't a wicked woman, she was—uh—"

"Wanton?"

"Yes. She felt horrible about what she had done, and what the consequences might have been for Rebecca. She died a year later. Influenza was only partly to blame."

"And then there was Catherine's third victim," I said.

He looked at me, surprised.

"Sarah. Your niece. I'd say it's a sure thing that Rebecca's disappearance and Sarah's murder are related."

Huge tears welled in the corners of his eyes, wobbled there for a second, and then threaded their way through the maze of furrows that formed his cheeks.

I turned discreetly away and studied the cornfield. We'd had a dry spring, and the crop was going to have to do some fancy growing if it was going to be knee-high by the Fourth of July.

If only it was already the Fourth. Sarah would be buried, I'd be married, and the aunties would be out of the house. Everything would be on track again, and I could settle down for a life of married bliss—except for two very obvious flies in the pie of my dreams.

Susannah, of course, was one of the flies. But she had been buzzing around the periphery of my happiness for as long as I could remember, and I was used to her. No, the fly that stood the greatest chance of tainting this pie was an eighty-year-old man with a guilty conscience and pockets full of nothing.

"Damn," I said. It was only the second time I'd ever used the word, so I didn't deserve getting caught.

"Pardon me?"

"Uh—well, Pops, I've been thinking."

"You've changed your mind about taking me in, haven't you? Well, I understand."

If only it was so simple. My Pooky Bear would never forgive me if I put his Pops out in the cold. The truth is, I would never forgive myself—no matter how much I wanted to do so with half of my heart. The wrong half, of course.

"No, Pops, like I said, I'm delighted that you'll be living with us. I changed my mind about waiting here for Aaron."

The relief on his face was one of my rewards for those times when the good half of my heart prevails. "I'm sure Aaron will only be a few minutes more."

"Yes, just a few minutes more. That's why I've decided to leave you here alone—if that's all right—and hoof it on back through the cornfields. After all, I've got on a comfortable pair of shoes and I know a shortcut."

"Ah, yes, so my son and I could have that talk."

"Yes, the talk."

But it had nothing to do with any talk. I needed the time to think, and what better place than a cornfield? Without cow pies and cats to dodge, without phones ringing off the hooks, without aunties and temperamental cooks, I might actually reach some much needed conclusions.

And I did.

10

Magdalena Yoder's Wedding Feast, from Soup to Nuts

Freni Hostetler's Wilted Dandelion Salad

The best dandelion leaves are gathered in the early spring before the plants have had a chance to bloom. Be sure that the plants have not been sprayed with toxins. If suitable dandelion leaves are not available, endive may be substituted.

5 or 6 cups of leaves, broken into bite-size pieces

Dressing:
4 slices bacon
bacon grease
1 tablespoon flour
1 cup sugar
½ teaspoon salt
½ teaspoon pepper
1/3 cup vinegar

1 cup water
2 hard-boiled eggs, peeled and sliced

Fry bacon until crisp. Remove from pan and crumble. Sprinkle flour over bacon grease remaining in pan and stir well. Add sugar, salt, pepper, vinegar, and water. Bring to a boil, stirring constantly. Pour hot liquid over salad greens and stir well. Garnish with egg slices and bacon bits.

Serves 4.

11

Walking home gave me plenty of time to think, but take my word for it, no matter how comfortable your shoes, don't walk six miles across cornfields in your Sunday dress—at least not in Pennsylvania. Our fields are anything but flat, and sometimes they are interrupted by streams and patches of brambly woods. By the time I staggered in the back door, I was covered with more scratches than a declawed tomcat and I had chafe marks in places my Pooky Bear had yet to see.

I would have tottered straight off for a long soak in my tub if it hadn't been for one of my Pooky Bear's relations. Auntie Veronica, she of the protruding proboscis and tiny feet, was sitting at the kitchen table, a dish towel knotted around both hands. She looked like she was going to strangle me with it.

"Just because Leah made lunch doesn't mean I'm going to wash dishes," she said.

"Of course not, dear. Speaking of which, how was it?"

"The roast was dry, the potatoes overdone, and the beans didn't have any flavor. I know Leah thinks she's a good cook, but I've seldom had worse."

I smiled charmingly. "Actually, I made the lunch. It only needed to be reheated when we got back from church. But as you can see, I'm just now getting back."

She looked me up and down. "Our little Aaron doesn't know what he's getting into, does he?" she clucked.

"He knows enough. By the way, where is he?"

"Beats me. Neither Aaron was here for lunch."

Ever the worrier, I felt a twinge of panic. Perhaps Aaron Senior had suffered a heart attack out there on the road by himself. Perhaps at that very moment my Aaron was sitting outside the intensive care unit of Bedford Hospital, blaming it all on me.

"You mean they didn't make it back from church?"

"Oh, they made it back all right," she snapped. "Popped in just for a second, though. Just long enough to say that they were skipping lunch because they had a lot to talk about. Imagine that!"

"Actually, I can."

I tottered past her and through to the dining room. It was deserted. Good Mennonites refrain from quilting on Sundays. Undoubtedly the rest of the Beeftrust were upstairs in their rooms, reading or napping. Whichever it was, they had their privacy, because the uncles—to a man—were sawing wood in the parlor. The faith of my fathers lived on still.

I should have been ravenous, but all I could think of was a long, hot bath. By the time I was through soaking I had probably absorbed enough water through my skin to fill me up. At any rate, as soon as I was dressed I called telephone information.

"For what city, please."

"Sarasota, Florida." It was a wild guess. For reasons I know not, Mennonites, and some Amish, are particularly fond of Sarasota.

"Go ahead, please."

"Yes, I'd like the number of a Jonas Weaver."

There was a long pause. "Do you have a middle initial, ma'am? I show six listings by that name."

I took down all six numbers and began with the first given me.

"Weavoh wesidence." The speaker couldn't have been more than three years old. "Jonas Weavoh speaking."

"Hello. Is your mommy home?"

"No, Mama died Fwiday night. Didn't they tell you that at chuch?"

"No, they didn't. I'm sorry."

"Why be sowee? She lived to see huh hundwedth buthday, didn't she?"

"She did? Say, the Jonas Weaver I'm looking for is originally from Hernia, Pennsylvania, and—"

"I'm not that Jonas," the pipsqueak squeaked. "Ahm fwum Geoge-uh!"

The second Jonas hailed from Intercourse, Pennsylvania. Did I want to know how the town got its name, he asked? I did not!

Not only was the third time the charm, but the man on the other end of the line was quite charming. "Guilty," he purred in response to my Hernia question.

"This isn't a trial, Mr. Weaver. It's just that I have something very important to tell you."

"Tell me, then, and please don't leave out a word. I could listen to you talk for hours."

Something wasn't right. So, to put it in terms my Aaron understands, I decided on a lateral pass to the left.

"Did I say the Jonas Weaver I'm looking for is from Hernia? How silly of me. The one I'm looking for lived in Hernia briefly, but he's really from Truss, Pennsylvania."

"Even guiltier," the pervert purred.

I hung up without telling him there wasn't such a place.

It wasn't until the sixth and last call that I reached a cantankerous old man with a scratchy voice. I knew instinctively that I had struck pay dirt. Through a series of snarls he informed me that I was the first person from Hernia to speak to him in almost twenty years.

"Then I'm sorry, Mr. Weaver, but I have some bad news for you from home."

"Yeah? First, how'd you find me?"

"I called directory information."

"Yeah?" He thought about that for a few minutes, no doubt marveling all the while. Most people either don't know such a service exists or else they're too cheap to pay the paltry sum it costs to use it. The PennDutch Inn is listed in the Bedford County phone book, but you'd be surprised how many folks say they can't find my number—especially when their business with me involves a cancellation.

"You there, Mr. Weaver?"

"All right, so you found me. Now, what's the bad news?"

"It's about your daughter, sir."

"I don't have a daughter, so don't give me that crap."

"Sarah!" I shouted, before he could hang up. "She's been found."

"What?"

"Your daughter Sarah's body has finally been found."

I expected the silence, but I didn't expect the tears. One more weeper and I was going to call it quits for the day. Still, I waited patiently as the minutes ticked by on my phone bill.

"Where?"

"On Aaron Miller's farm. The funeral—"

"Where on the farm?"

"The root cellar."

"Buried under the floor?"

It was a reasonable possibility, I suppose, but something that hadn't occurred to me.

"No, sir. It isn't very pleasant, I'm afraid."

"Death seldom is."

I breathed deeply. "She was in a barrel of sauerkraut."

"My God," he said quietly.

"Mr. Weaver, if you come home for the funeral, you're welcome to stay with me. I own an inn right across from the Miller farm."

"Who'd you say you were again? Because there isn't any inn across from that farm."

I outlined who I was and how the inn came about. He seemed satisfied. At least satisfied enough for me to ask him a few more questions.

"You had to be awfully sure, Mr. Weaver, that your wife and daughter were dead. I mean, in order to cut yourself off like that for so long. If you don't mind my asking, how could you be so sure?"

The ensuing silence was so long I thought he'd hung up. "Hello? Hello?"

"I'm here." It was barely a whisper.

"Mr. Weaver, I assure you that you can trust me. I won't tell a soul, if that's what you want."

"I have your word?"

"Absolutely."

"Because of her diary," he blurted.

"Whose diary? Rebecca's?"

"Sarah's. I read it after she disappeared. She wrote in it that she had seen her mother killed. She knew that the killer saw her, and she believed she was going to be next."

It was my turn to practice that elusive virtue. "You did tell the police about this," I said at last.

"No, I did not."

I felt like I was dealing with a wily, feral animal that I had taken it upon myself to tame. At any moment it could bolt back into the woods and I might never see it again.

"I'm sure the police would have been able to solve the murders if they had seen the diary." I said it kindly, I really did.

"I couldn't show it to them." It was like he was wanting me to draw him further out of the woods.

"Why not?"

"I just couldn't." The animal had coyly taken one step backward.

I thought about Susannah's diary, which she keeps locked and under a pile of blankets in a locked chest. No doubt some of the things written in there would curl the hair on even Satan's head.

"Were there things written in there that were private?" I asked delicately.

He cleared his throat. "Yeah."

"So private that it was more important to keep them secret than to find your wife and daughter's killer?"

"Yeah."

"Do you still have the diary, Mr. Weaver?"

He hesitated. "I think so."

"Then I'd like to make a suggestion, if I might. Please reread your daughter's diary. A lot of things have changed in the last twenty years. Maybe the things in there aren't so—"

"Morality never changes," he said.

"True, but people judge things less harshly now."

He said nothing.

"I could make sure that the Hernia police look only at the parts that pertain to the murder."

"How can you do that?" The animal had stepped boldly out into the open. It was up to me to coax it to my hand.

"Because the current chief of police is my dear cousin. We go back a long ways."

There was at least a kernel of truth in that, and it was for a good cause. And even though Melvin wouldn't cross the street to acknowledge our kinship, I had ways to make him sing and dance on cue. After all, Melvin had made the gross mistake of dating my sister. If Jonas Weaver thought his daughter's diary was revealing, just wait till he and the world got a look at Susannah's.

"Well, I will think about it," he said.

"You are at least coming to the funeral, aren't you?"

"Yeah. I would like to do that."

"I mean, she was your daughter. Feel free to make any or all of the arrangements."

"No, I'd rather somebody else did that. Would you do that? Please?"

"Of course." The fact was, I already had—everything except for the exact time. "And will you agree to stay at the inn?"

"Yeah, I'll stay."

"Good. In fact, why don't you just come on ahead as soon as you can? Give me a call when you've booked a flight, and I'll send Aaron Junior out to the Pittsburgh airport to get you."

He agreed that's what he'd do and we said our goodbyes.

I must have slept for hours, because the shadows were long outside my windows when I woke up. Unfortunately I had broken one of my cardinal rules about napping, because my head ached, my eyes hurt, and I felt as crabby as a constipated hen. Just lying there was agony enough, but the persistent knocking on my door bordered on excruciating.

"Go away!"

The door opened. "Aha! I thought you were in there."

It was my Pooky Bear, bearing a tray of supper. I should have been delighted.

"Ugh." I shielded my eyes with my arm as Aaron turned on the light.

"Same back at you," he said cheerily. "Look what I brought. Here we have some chicken salad, a little cottage cheese, some spinach—"

"Please, Aaron. I feel like I've been run over by a combine."

"Well, you don't look like it. You look just as beautiful as ever to me. Even more so."

"I do?"

"You look like a dream come true to me."

I sat up and surreptitiously smoothed the hair back from my face. Of course I was dressed, I just didn't have my shoes on.

"Why, Aaron Miller, how sweet you can be."

"And this is just the beginning."

I inspected the tray closer. Suddenly I was ravenous. Even the bearded irises Aaron had stuck in a juice glass looked delicious.

"Go on and eat," Aaron said, "while I tell you just how much I adore you."

I did his bidding. Who says I'm not a cooperative person? "Never pass up a free meal," Mama always said. Of course, this wasn't a free meal, coming as it did straight out of my kitchen, but Mama had never been lavished with sweet sentiments or she would have given advice on accepting those as well.

"I just can't thank you enough for what you did," my Pooky Bear said.

I swallowed a bite of chicken salad that may have been just a trifle too large. "What did I do? Tell me, and I'll do it again."

He laughed heartily. "As if you didn't know! Well, that's my Magdalena for you. Always cracking jokes."

"Yeah, that's me."

"Pops adores you too, you know that? It's going to do him a world of good to move out of that big old house and in with us."

"Oh, he told you that?"

"I never would have asked you, you know. I would have hated to live with my in-laws. Theoretically, of course. I'm sure your folks would have been very pleasant to be around."

"Just don't bet on it. What all did your father say?"

Aaron shook his head. "I still can't get over it. That whole flat tire thing was all a setup for my big surprise."

"And were you?"

"Yeah, but I shouldn't have been. I should have known how sweet you are. Asking Pops to move in with us—no, begging him, he said."

"Oh, he did?"

"And then asking him if it was all right to call him Pops!"

"Well." I shrugged magnanimously.

"And then the icing on the cake!"

"There's cake too?" I pushed the iris arrangement aside but found no such thing.

"As if you didn't know! Promising to name our son Aaron Weaver the Third was the biggest gift you could have given to a man his age."

I dropped my fork. "Our son?"

"Our son. You do want children, don't you?"

"Aaron, I'm forty-four!"

"Forty-two."

"Forty-four," I wailed.

He shrugged nonchalantly. "So—this is the nineteen-nineties. Women your age are always having babies."

"But a first baby?"

"There's a first time for everything," he said blithely.

"Then have it yourself," I almost said. Instead, I picked the supper tray clean. After all, according to Aaron, I was soon going to be eating for two.

12

I have never been a big fan of Mondays. Actually, as far as I'm concerned, the week starts a downward plunge around noon on Sunday and doesn't begin its next ascent until noon on Friday. Today, however, I had the memory of my Pooky Bear's adoration to sustain me.

Aaron and Pops, as I shall hereafter refer to him, had left early for the Pittsburgh airport to collect Jonas Weaver. Jonas had called late the night before, accepting my invitation and announcing a ten o'clock arrival. Since it is two and a half hours from the airport to Hernia, I didn't expect them back until after lunch. As for the Beeftrust and their consorts, they had decided, en masse, to pay a sentimental visit to old Hernia High and then have a picnic up on Stucky Ridge. I told Freni to take the morning off, and I let Susannah sleep. It was time to get down to some serious business.

Hernia, Pennsylvania, population 1,528, is a nice place to live, but you wouldn't want to visit there. As Susannah says, the only thing to do is watch moss grow and pick your toes. Actually, Susannah's is a cruder version, but you get my drift. At any rate, our police force, which was recently upgraded to three (two full-time, one part) doesn't get a lot of business on Monday mornings. Therefore, I expected to get their full attention, if not cooperation. I knew from experience that Chief of Police Melvin Stoltzfus was usually on duty Monday mornings. Foolishly I decided to take my chances and not call first. And as usual, Melvin, the manic mantis, tried my patience sorely.

"I'm off duty," he said, speaking to me from behind his desk.

"But you're here."

"So are you, Yoder, and you're not on duty."

"But this is your office, and you're in."

"And since this is my office, Yoder, I don't have to explain my actions."

"Who is on duty, then?"

"No one. Not until ten."

"Come on, Melvin, this is very important."

He rotated an eye to the clock on the wall. "Come back in an hour. We'll talk then."

"What will I do for an hour, Melvin? I don't want to drive home and back."

"Shop," he said.

With that, Melvin propped his feet up on his desk, clasped his bony hands over the tiniest of potbellies, and was out like a light. I decided to take him at his word. I would be back in precisely an hour. At that time we would talk, even if it meant having to throw a pitcher of ice water in his face first.

Hernia has two stores: Yoder's Corner Market and Miller's Feed Store. The former is overpriced and understocked, and the latter caters to stock—livestock, that is.

I own two dairy cows, Matilda and Bessie. In the spring they need very little from the feed store, so I decided to while away my hour at Yoder's Corner Market. But unless I chanced upon an exceptional bargain, I wouldn't buy anything. Sam Yoder, the proprietor, is my father's first cousin once removed, but I still have to pay full price. Even Sam's seventy- three-year-old mother has to pay full price, and he lives with her!

Sam was the closest thing I had to a suitor in high school, and if it hadn't been for my pining over Aaron and he over Dorothy Gillman (a Methodist!) we might have ended up life partners. I, of course, do not regret the way things turned out, but I don't think the same thing can be said for Sam. To please Dorothy, Sam became a Methodist, but it has not been a happy marriage. What mixed marriage is? Dorothy is far too worldly to suit Sam, and loose with the change besides. I hear she once spent over a hundred dollars buying curtains at the Kmart in Bedford, when she could have made them herself! Sam almost divorced her over that, which would have been wrong but certainly understandable.

"Hi, Sam, what's up?"

Sam glowered at me. "Your beefy relatives just swept through here like a herd of buffalo. Messed everything up and bought almost nothing. Claimed my prices were too high."

"They are."

"Well, they're not going to find anything else to picnic on in Hernia."

"Not unless they try the feed store."

We both laughed. "Sam, how well do you remember Sarah Weaver?"

His face darkened again. "Jonas and Rebecca's daughter?"

"The one. I suppose by now you've heard."

"It's all over town, Magdalena. A terrible way to die—drowning in a barrel of cider."

"It was sauerkraut. And I don't think she drowned. I think she was dead before she went in."

"Still, what a tragic waste."

I left that line alone. Sam is too closely related to have meant it in the morally correct way.

"Did you know her well, Sam?"

A dreamy look crept across his face. "No, not Sarah. Too young. But I remember her mother."

"Oh?" I asked cautiously.

"Yeah, all the guys remember her. She was—uh—"

"Pretty?"

"Built like a brick shithouse."

"Shame on you, Sam Yoder! A Methodist tongue!" I chided him gently. "So, she was easy on your eyes. What else do you remember?"

"She wore very short skirts and tight sweaters."

"She was a Mennonite, Sam. I'm sure she did no such thing."

"Ask any man our age. Mrs. Weaver was what you wished all your dates looked like."

I would have slapped Sam, but dozens of generations of pacifist forebears have left their genetic imprint on me. Besides, I had just spotted a hickory- smoked ham that had been mispriced to my advantage. Sam does not have a scanner, and if I kept him distracted—in a non-combative way—the ham could be mine for a song.

"That's very interesting," I said pleasantly. "I mean, the Beeftrust are not exactly drop-dead gorgeous. And I mean that in the nicest way."

"No argument there. But Mrs. Weaver wasn't like the others. She was the youngest, I think. Kept herself in good shape. Could really turn heads."

I let Sam ring up the twenty-dollar ham for two dollars. Then, not feeling the least bit guilty, I deposited a quarter in the charity box by the register. If I knew Sam, the two bits would never reach the big-eyed children with the sunken cheeks. As soon as I got home, however, I would mail them half of my eighteen-dollar profit.

"Well, from what I hear, her sister Lizzie was quite a looker too."

Sam made the same face Susannah makes when she tastes Freni's homemade liverwurst. "I don't know much about her. She was older. Grown-up-looking, you know."

"Did you and your drooling cronies ever make a pass at Sarah's mother?"

He blanched white as bleached cake flour. "Naw, I mean, we were just kids, and she was a grown-up too. She just didn't look like the rest. Besides, her husband wouldn't stand for it."

"Oh?" For talkers like Sam, an arched eyebrow and a rounded mouth are all they need for fuel.

"That man was downright weird. Real quiet all the time. Too quiet. Like a snake, if you know what I mean."

I nodded, the "oh" and the arch still in place.

"He used to come into this store a lot when it was my daddy's. I'd see him then. He gave me the heebie-jeebies. He was always staring at you, with eyes that never blinked. Like I said, he reminded me of a snake."

A customer came in then. Norah Hall is the nosiest woman this side of the Delaware. She also has it in for me. Something about it being my fault her pudgy prepubescent daughter didn't get to be a movie star that time a Hollywood company rented my inn for a few weeks. At any rate, Norah was sure to peek into my bag, see the mispriced ham, and squeal on me. Sam then would ban me from his store for life, depriving me of one of my few pleasures, and the big-eyed waifs would go hungry.

"That is such a flattering color on you," I said to Norah and fled. Always compliment your enemies before fleeing. It throws them off track every time.

Melvin was still asleep when I returned. I didn't have a pitcher of ice water at my disposal, but it was a simple matter to push his feet off the desk. The silly man jumped up and saluted me.

"Sir! Private Melvin Stoltzfus reporting to duty, sir!"

"At ease, private," I said kindly.

He rubbed his giant orbs with both fists. "That isn't funny, Magdalena. I worked Zelda's shift last night—she's sick. That was the first chance I had to close my eyes since yesterday morning. I guess I fell asleep and was dreaming. You know, I could arrest you for breaking and entering. And assaulting a police officer."

"No, you couldn't."

"Want to bet?"

I opened my pocketbook and whipped out a little pink book with a gold clasp. "You'd lose, dear."

His eyes took turns inspecting the pink book. "What's that?"

"Susannah's diary. The unabridged version."

He sat down again as abruptly as if he'd been pushed.

"What is it you want, Yoder?"

"Your official cooperation."

"Are you blackmailing me?"

"The diary is pink, dear. Inside, however, it's red hot."

He tried bluffing, a mistake for male mantises. The female gets them every time.

"So? Sex is the national pastime. Nobody's going to care."

Tamar Myers

97

"The taxpayers will care."

He turned whiter than Cousin Sam had. "Get to the point, Yoder."

Allow me to assure you that I had not even skimmed Susannah's diary, much less read it. I knew that she kept the book under a pair of black lace panties in her left bottom dresser drawer, but I had no idea where she kept the key. However, on more than one occasion, Susannah has let slip references to things that Melvin did, or places that he took her to, that he had no business doing in a city-owned car.

"Like I said, I simply want your cooperation, Melvin."

"Details, then, please." He said it almost politely.

I pulled up a chair that had been wasting its time in a corner. "I know where there's proof that Rebecca Weaver— Sarah's mother—was killed. Proof that Sarah saw it happen and her life was in danger when she disappeared."

"Where is this proof?"

"In a diary."

His mouth opened and closed, and he began madly mashing his mandibles. "This is ridiculous," he said at last. "I may have had the hots for Sarah's mother—all the boys did—but I never told Susannah that. And I certainly didn't kill Mrs. Weaver."

Dawn came slowly to my aging brain, but it brought a smile with it. "I'm not talking about you, or this diary at the moment. I'm talking about another diary. One that belonged to our victim herself."

"I'm not in it?" He sounded almost disappointed.

"I'm sure you are," I said kindly. "But I'm also sure you are not the one she saw kill her mother," I added soothingly.

But was I? Jonas wouldn't tell me who the killer was over the phone. But of course it couldn't have been Melvin.

The man was as irritating as a mosquito up your ear, but he wasn't a killer. There wasn't a violent bone in his body—or was there?

Susannah had said once that he slapped her. There is never an excuse for hitting a woman—or any human being—but that's only a fine and dandy theory when Susannah's in the picture. Susannah's talent for lying aside, that woman could provoke Mother Teresa into picking up an Uzi and spraying a roomful of sleeping babies. Melvin may have slapped Susannah, but even if he had, the man wasn't a cold-blooded killer. I would stake my inn on that.

"Where is this diary?" Melvin demanded. "It's police business, and I want you to hand it over immediately."

I smiled patiently. "It's on its way here from the Pittsburgh airport, dear. But, like I said, I want your cooperation."

He stared at me with both eyes, quite a feat of cooperation in itself. "Details, Yoder."

"The diary belongs to Sarah's father now. Jonas Weaver. As you surely know, diaries can contain some very personal information, and this one does. Information that has nothing to do with the case. It—"

"It's up to me to decide that, isn't it?" he snapped.

I held up Susannah's plastic-bound secrets. "Ah, ah, ah! No, you don't. That's why I brought up the subject of this little gem. It's very important to Jonas that we read only the parts that pertain to the murder."

"We?"

"You and I, of course. Who else is going to keep an eye on you?"

"The hell you say, Yoder. If Mr. Weaver wants to sit beside me and turn the pages, that's all right, but you're not going to be anywhere around. The last thing I need is for you to get some crazy ideas from what's in there and then nm off and try to play hero."

"Moi?"

But it was no use trying to act innocent. Melvin knew from experience that I am not one to sit idly by while the police take their own sweet time with things.

"Let me put it this way, Yoder. If you get in my way at all, I'm going to arrest you for obstructing a police officer in the pursuit of his duty."

It sounded like a bogus charge, but it didn't matter. As long as Melvin did the job we paid him to do, then I would stand back, and gladly. I had a million things still to do for the wedding, and none of them had anything to do with solving twenty-year-old murders.

"Pursue your duty, then." Before I left his office, I waved the pink diary at him one more time for good measure.

13

I drove up to Stucky Ridge without a picnic lunch. Most people do. The crest of Stucky Ridge is the highest point for miles around, and while it offers wonderful picnic views, most of its visitors are teenagers who park along the rim and do everything but look at the scenery. They, of course, come at night.

Stucky Ridge is what we in the East often call a mountain, but what folks in the West might call a wrinkle, or a hill at most. According to geologists, Stucky Ridge was once at the bottom of a primeval swamp, and as a consequence was blessed with a collection of swamp creatures which somehow got compressed and turned into coal. Clarence Stucky, who owned most of the ridge, strip-mined the coal and then turned the denuded mountain over to the town of Hernia for use as a city park. That was thirty years ago, and thanks to the valiant efforts of the Greater Hernia Plant and Pick It Garden Club, the scars left by the strip mining have been concealed, if not healed.

The north end of the ridge, however, was never mined. Since the days of the first white settlers it has been continuously inhabited by Amish and Mennonites other than the

Stucky family, and Clarence was unable to strip the coal out from under them. The current residents may be confined by a wrought iron fence and their view obscured by a copse, but they aren't about to move. The official name for this little community is the Settlers' Cemetery, and that's where my parents are buried.

According to a document filed at city hall and on record in Harrisburg, the descendants of Hernia's first settlers may be interred on Stucky Ridge in perpetuity. Five male Stucky ancestors signed this document, and there it is, in black and white for all current-day Stuckys to see. Now that the entire ridge has been deeded over to the city it is no longer a problem, but I can remember the day when Amish buggies and Mennonite cars encircled the cemetery to keep Clarence's bulldozers from coming any closer.

At any rate, both Mama and Papa are descended from Hernia's earliest settlers, in so many ways it would make your head spin to try and keep them all straight. Suffice it to say that Papa's main connection was his great-great-great-great-great grandfather Christian Yoder, and Mama's her great-great-great- great-great grandfather Joseph Hochstetler. Those are the names that appear first on the official document. But since no pioneer could have done it without his wife (certainly not produced descendants), I feel it is only right to mention that Christian's wife was Barbara Hooley and Joseph's wife was Anna Blank.

At the top of the ridge the gravel road splits, with the right fork turning off to the parking areas and picnic tables. As I continued on toward Settlers' Cemetery, I could see among the parked cars the ones driven up by the Beeftrust. The hostess in me felt a sudden urge to stop and inquire politely about their lunch, but I repressed it. They were big girls, after all, quite capable of fending for themselves. I was the one who needed help.

It is a small cemetery, and despite their connections, my parents are having to share far closer quarters than they could possibly have shared in real life. Mama always chided me about walking across people's graves, so I had to zigzag down the narrow, grassy aisles, and when I got there I was very careful not to put the stadium seat down on Mama's turf. Papa, I knew, wouldn't mind my legs stretched out above him.

"It's like this," I began. "You've really messed things up for me, you know. Of course you couldn't help getting rear-ended by a milk tanker, but you didn't have to die. I wouldn't have died and left two helpless children to fend for themselves.

"All right, so I wasn't exactly a child, but Susannah was. Not in years, maybe, but you know what I mean. How did you expect me to raise her by myself, when you two couldn't even do the job right?"

I clamped my hand over my mouth. "I didn't mean that, Mama. Please don't start turning over in your grave like you always threatened."

I waited a few minutes, and when there were no tremors I continued. "I'm supposed to get married Saturday. But Sarah's murder—well, her discovery, at least—has ruined everything. Couldn't you have stopped it? I mean, don't you have any influence up there at all?"

My hand found my mouth again. It wasn't the first time I'd come close to blasphemy. But that time back in my fifth grade Sunday school class when I referred to God as She, I was under the influence of a double dose of cold medicine. Still, I said a silent prayer before addressing Papa's plot.

"You always said I was your special girl. You were supposed to give me away," I wailed.

"And you," I said to Mama's matted mound, "were supposed to help me with the preparations. You know, the girl stuff. But where are you?" I wailed.

"Mum rig hah," Mama said.

I jumped two feet in the air, which is quite a feat when one starts from a sitting position. It's a wonder my heart didn't burst out of my chest and go soaring over the edge of Stucky Ridge.

"Whad din minta scary ah," Mama said calmly. Her poor diction I attributed to six feet of earth.

I tried to stand up, but I couldn't move my legs off the top of Papa's grave. Perhaps he had a hold on them.

"Ins onee mee, Magdalena."

I heard my name clearly. Mama sounded closer as well.

"Yes, Mama, it's me," I said quickly. "Please don't be mad at me. I'm sorry for what I said. It's just that—"

Suddenly Mama was standing right beside me. But I hadn't seen her actually come out of the grave, and unless she had access to a back door, something was clearly wrong. Besides, the apparition looked nothing like I remembered Mama.

Mama had a beaked nose and dark, flashing eyes. The ghost had a long, pointed nose and faded blue eyes. Frankly, the ghost was dressed in the same drab dresses Mama always wore—before she liberalized and discovered the joy of pants— but unlike Mama, the ghost had huge bosoms and tiny, child-like hands.

"Auntie Magdalena!" I cried. "I didn't see you coming. You nearly scared me to death!"

Auntie Magdalena whimpered and mumbled a few phrases, and I discovered that by watching her lips closely I was able to follow along.

"I got bored with the picnic," she mumbled. "All I ever hear is how Vonnie and Rudy bought this or went there, and which movies Lizzie and Manasses saw. And Leah—you'd think the world revolved around her cooking."

"It is rather good," I said carelessly.

Auntie Magdalena whimpered a few things it's best not to repeat. "You'd think Elias and I didn't even exist," she added.

I thought that one over carefully. When you wear size eleven shoes, putting your foot in your mouth can be a mite uncomfortable.

"You don't suppose it has to do with, uh—"

"Race?"

"Yes."

"Absolutely not. When I first started dating Elias, my sisters couldn't wait to put their hands on him. I mean that figuratively, of course."

"Of course. Rebecca too, I suppose."

Auntie Magdalena looked at me like I had just told her that not only was the moon made of cheese but it was a nice imported Gouda.

"Becca was not like the others at all."

"A virtual saint, I suppose." The sarcasm just slipped out.

"Give me a break," Auntie Magdalena mumbled. "I know it's wrong to speak ill of the dead—especially in a cemetery—but she was twice as bad as the others. Threw herself at anyone in pants. And in those days that meant men."

I was going to have to take a crash course in face reading. "You mean she flirted?"

" 'Flirted' is the word you'd use when talking to a preacher. Flirted, ha! Becca was, uh—"

"Horny?" I know, it is a horrible word, but Susannah uses it, and frankly it seems to suit her. If Becca had been anything at all like Susannah, then everything Uncle Jonas had told me was suspect.

"That's what she was, all right. It was shameful. And it didn't stop after she was married, either. Poor Jonas, we always said."

"Who's we?"

"Everyone."

"I see. What about Catherine, Aaron Senior's wife?"

"What about her?"

"What was she like?"

"Catherine was my best friend, and as decent a woman as you could hope to find."

I chewed on that for a while. The truth has as many versions as there are tongues, but surely Auntie Magdalena had seen through her friend. Even Aaron Senior had recognized his wife's shortcomings.

"What do you think about Uncle Jonas?" I asked at last.

Auntie Magdalena bent over so her face was just inches from mine. Clearly she didn't want me to miss a word.

"I think Jonas killed his wife, that's what I think. And believe me, he had plenty of reason."

With some difficulty Auntie Magdalena righted herself and without another whimper, or mumbled word, wound her way through the cemetery and out the rusted wrought iron gate. I was alone again, with no one but Mama and Papa, and the shells of my ancestors. I began to cry.

Uncle Jonas was sitting by himself on the front porch of the inn when I drove up. There were no other cars in the drive, so I assumed that the Beeftrust had found another memory lane to follow and that Aaron had gone home to his father. As for Susannah, odds were she was still in bed, although there was a good chance she had at least turned over since I'd left.

For some reason Uncle Jonas in the flesh intimidated me. Perhaps it was the staring eyes that he was noted for. Perhaps it was because he was so tidy. I had the feeling he measured the length of his cuticles before and after he did his nails. There wasn't a hair on his head out of place, and not a nub of a whisker to be seen on his cheeks. The only other man I'd ever known to be so exacting in his neatness was my ninth grade algebra teacher, Mr. Rouck.

Mr. Rouck may have been neat, but he wasn't nice. By the end of the first semester I was envying my Amish neighbors who didn't have to go to school beyond the eighth grade. By the end of the year I was envying my Baptist friends who believed that at least some violence was justified by the Bible.

"Welcome to the PennDutch Inn," I called out gaily. Forced cheer is one of my strong points.

"Hello." I recalled the scratchy voice I'd heard on the phone. It was totally at odds with his appearance, but it made perfect sense. Mr. Rouck had had a voice that scratched glass.

I settled myself in a rocker next to his and cradled my purse in my lap.

"You have a good flight?"

He stared at me with eyes that were flat and gray, like pebbles plucked from a stream and allowed to dry.

"Cut out the small talk, please. I have decided to show the police Sarah's diary, but on one condition."

"Which is?"

"That Leah Troyer not be allowed to come to the funeral."

I stifled a gasp with my purse, bruising my nose in the process. "Our Leah?"

"The very one. Leader of the Beeftrust."

That was news to me. Leah had a loud voice, but she didn't seem like the leading type. I would have pegged fashionable Lizzie or crabby old Veronica for that role. And, of course, Magdalena didn't count.

"Well, I'm no expert on church policy," I said carefully, "but I always thought funerals were open to the public."

"There can be private burials," he rasped. "For family members only."

'But Leah is family. Sarah was her niece."

The flat eyes regarded me soberly, beneath eyebrows that had been precisely trimmed. "When one does what Leah did, then one is no longer family."

I held my purse at the ready. "What did she do?"

"My little girl went to her aunt for help, and she refused."

"You mean Sarah asked Leah for help? Something to do with her mother's killer?"

He nodded. "It's all there, in her diary."

We rocked in silence for a while. He was undoubtedly grieving; I was sorting things out. I needed Uncle Jonas's cooperation, but I couldn't promise to keep Leah away from the funeral, no matter what was in that diary. On the other hand, it was his daughter's funeral, and it really was up to him who should or should not attend. Besides, in this case the chicken definitely came before the egg. After we showed the diary to chicken Melvin, what was to stop me from going back on my word about Leah? Assuming, of course, that by that time I didn't agree with Uncle Jonas.

"Okay, you show the diary to the police, and I'll tell Leah she can't come to the funeral."

"No deal. You tell her first, and then we see about the police."

"You tell her yourself. It's your daughter's funeral."

He stared at me. If he had been Mr. Rouck, I could have expected my algebra grade to go down a letter.

"Look," I said, "the important thing is that we catch Sarah's killer, right? Punishing Leah is a secondary issue."

"Leah is my daughter's killer," he said quietly. His voice was remarkably clear.

14

"What? You can't be serious!"
He slowly pulled a small red book from underneath his rocker cushion. "It's in here. It's all in the diary."

"Let me see." I reached for it automatically.

He tucked the book back under the cushion. "I've decided not to show it to you."

"What?"

"I've decided that this police friend of yours is the only one who needs to see it. It's better for my daughter's memory that way."

I hadn't counted on that. I hadn't for a second considered the possibility that Melvin would see the diary, and I wouldn't. That was like letting a monkey loose in a secret munitions factory. Privacy might be preserved, but the whole place was liable to blow up.

"Uh—Chief Stoltzfus is really swamped at the moment. At times like this he appreciates my helping him out. Why don't I read the diary for him—only the pertinent parts, of course—and summarize it?"

"Bull," he rasped. Such a crude word from such an immaculate man.

"Look, Mr. Weaver"—calling him "Uncle Jonas" seemed too intimate—"whether you believe me or not, I'm on your side. Your daughter was my sister's best friend. Susannah has been deeply affected by this, and frankly, so have I. I'm supposed to get married on Saturday, and I'll be damned if I'll have a murder investigation hanging over our heads to screw things up."

This time his stare was less belligerent. "Your mother ever hear you talk like that?"

"No, and she never will. My mother's dead. You'd know that if you'd bothered to keep in touch with folks here."

He glanced around, as if seeing his surroundings for the first time. "I'd forgotten how nice it is here. How peaceful. And real."

"Real?"

"Back home—I mean, in Florida—nothing is as it seems. The folks there aren't from there, even the trees and flowers they grow are from someplace else. And the land—you dig down two feet and there isn't any dirt at all, just limestone. They say that if the polar ice cap melts just a foot, there won't be any Florida at all. All the pink plastic flamingos will be washed away by the waves. No more shuffleboard courts, either."

"Is that so?" It was comforting to know that my Pennsylvania mountain valley had its particular advantages.

He nodded. "Maybe I'll stay a while. Know of any rooms to rent in the area?"

"Is the pope Catholic?"

He actually smiled. "I'm afraid your place would be out of my league, Miss Yoder. I was thinking more like a rooming house in town."

"Delores Brown sometimes has rooms to rent. She's a Methodist, though, so her rooms don't have a theme. And she's nosier than a roomful of reporters. Still, I hear she's reasonable."

The truth be known, Delores can hardly give her rooms away. I should feel sorry for the woman, because before the PennDutch hit it big, she was the only game in town. But face it—folks don't want just a place to sleep anymore, they want entertainment. If they're real discriminating, that entertainment is atmosphere with an attitude.

"She in the book?" he asked.

"Yes. But the poor dear's hard of hearing and almost never answers her phone. If you want, I'll drive over there this afternoon and ask her."

"Thank you."

He closed his eyes for a minute, and I thought maybe he had gone to sleep. Mennonite uncles are capable of falling into deep, coma-like sleep in less time than it takes to clear the dinner table. Therefore it took me by surprise when he reached behind him to get the diary and then held it out to me.

"Okay," he said, his eyes still closed. "You can look at the diary. But not those parts that are taped shut. And no showing it to anyone else."

"Thank you," I said.

I had never been so disappointed in my life. It was no big deal to buckle the taped pages and read what was written on them. Out of respect for the dead— and Uncle Jonas—I will not tell you what was written between those taped pages. Suffice it to say, Sarah had nothing approaching Susannah's behavior, even at that age. Shoot, had I been dating Aaron Miller back then, and not Sam Yoder, I might have done those things myself—except for that open-mouth kissing. That's going too far.

Then I read the part I was meant to read. Suddenly the sixteen-year-old Sarah I knew, with the long blond hair and paisley hairband, was standing in front of me. She and Susannah were giggling, no doubt making fun of me for something. Trying to get a rise out of me. I snapped at them and they pranced out of the room, laughing loudly. The next thing I knew, Sarah had dark hollows around her eyes. Her hair looked like it hadn't been combed for days. She clung to Susannah like a bean plant to a pole. Then she was gone.

I closed the diary and hugged it to my chest. Tears were streaming down my cheeks. Sarah Weaver had come alive in those pages, and I felt ashamed for having pried further than I needed to. However, there was nothing in what I had read that pointed to her mother's killer. And as for Auntie Leah— who hasn't sometimes been too busy doing some task to tolerate an interruption? What she did was lamentable, but surely not a crime. Here, judge for yourself. (To be honest, I had to straighten some of the grammar and correct the spelling mistakes. Although pretty girls can be very bright, Sarah Weaver was not one of them.)

July 2nd... drove to Hernia where Mama grew up. Only have to be here for a week, thank God. This place is zilchville. We're actually on a farm, if you can believe that. Cows and everything. Uncle Aaron is real nice, but Auntie Catherine—Mama thinks she's trashy and she's right. Met a girl who lives across the road. Her name is Susannah. She's real cool and you'd like her (but not too much, I hope!). Mama says I can take her with us to the picnic. I wish you could come. I'm going to miss Harry. Harry, I miss you! OOOOXXXX!

July 3rd... the other aunties and uncles arrived today. Uncle Elias is black! I almost forgot. Cool! Auntie Magdalena is weird though. You can't understand what she says. I don't remember Auntie Leah being so tall (ha!). She has no neck! She looks silly next to Uncle Sol, who looks like Elmer Fudd if you ask me. Auntie Vonnie is still crabby (even Mama says she is!). But Uncle Rudy is gross. Tell you later, Harry. Yuck, yuck, yuck! Oops! I almost forgot the Bloughs. They're cool. Auntie Lizzie wears makeup!!! Oodles of it! (Susannah does too, and she's going to show me how!) Don't worry about the boy cousins, Harry. They are all WEIRDOS!!! OOOOXXXX times ten!

July 4th... picnic up on Stucky Ridge. Great view. No cute boys (I told you not to worry, Harry!). Just cousins. Yuck! Thank God Susannah was there. We threw pine cones at the mean boy cousins. Mama went to the cemetery by herself. When she came back she was crying. Auntie Vonnie and Uncle Rudy got into another fight again. So what else is new? Sorry, but I think Auntie Magdalena is strange! Reminds me of a lost puppy. Get this—Hernia doesn't have fireworks, they have a revival meeting! The preacher was a weird man who sweated a lot and played the accordion. Gross! Susannah brought her boy friend and a "date" for me. Don't worry, Harry, this guy was GROSS, GROSS, GROSS! His name is Melvin Stiltfuzz, or something like that. It was gross just sitting by him. He tried to hold my hand and I pinched him. OOOOXXXX

July 5th... spent most of the day across at Susannah's house. She has a real mean older sister named Magdalena. Susannah showed me how to put on makeup. You'd love it, Harry! Not the makeup—I mean me in it, of course! When I went back to Uncle Aaron's I found Mama in the field (pasture?) by herself. She was crying again. She wouldn't tell me what was bothering her, but I think I know. It's something really gross! If Daddy ever found out—well, he better not! I made Mama laugh with my makeup. I thought she'd be mad, but she wasn't. She made me wash it off before supper though. She said only Auntie Lizzie would under-stand. Oh, that stupid boy Melvin tried to come by after supper. I told him to take a flying leap—so you see, you shouldn't worry, Harry. OOOOXXXX

July 6th—Susannah and I made her sister drive us into Bedford for a matinee. Magdalena wouldn't come in with us. Says she's never seen a movie. Can you believe that? Susannah likes Robert Redford— but he's so old! I like John Travolta. But not better than you, Harry! After the movie we went someplace for pizza. That stupid Melvin was there again. What a jerk! Auntie Leah made supper tonight. She's a good cook—bet-ter than Mama—but I was too full to eat any. Mama didn't eat either. She was upset about something. The same thing I think. It's just too gross. Daddy would die if he knew. I hope you haven't forgotten to feed Wiggles. Thanks for taking care of him! OOOOXXXX

July 7th... Auntie Vonnie is crabby, but that's no excuse, if you ask me. Maybe someday I'll tell you. Did you know that the Fikes have five children, but they only brought two. The others were old enough to stay home. I wish I had! They say they're black, but they don't look like it to me. Well, Betty does. She's the baby of all the cousins. I think she's ten. Anyway, they're the only ones stay-ing here, besides us—and Uncle Aaron and Auntie Catherine of course! The others are staying with other relatives at night, but in the daytime they all hang out here. Not me! I spend as much time across the road at Susannah's as I can. I want to stay there over night, but Mama won't let me. She says she needs me. She doesn't, you know! Be glad you're not here. Oh, to¬night was that stu-pid anniversary dinner for Uncle Aaron and Auntie Catherine. What a crock! All they ever do is fight, and what's so special about twenty- five years anyway? Someday we'll be married longer than that. OOOOXXX

There were no more entries until two days after the Weavers were scheduled to go home. Clearly they hadn't.

July 11th... I still can't believe it! It was the worst thing I ever saw! It was worse than the movies. Oh, Mama, what happened after that?????? Where are you, Mama? I know you didn't run off to the Poconos. That was Auntie Catherine. Everybody knows that. She is just trash, like you said. Mama, I can't tell anybody because I'm afraid! What should I do??? I can't even tell Susannah. She would never believe it. Not in a million years. Please God, make my Mama alright. If you do, I promise not to wear makeup anymore. I won't even go to movies. I won't kiss Harry again—not until we're married anyway.

July 12th... Mama come back! Where did you go? I should have done something to stop you. I'm stronger than I look, Mama! Mama, I love you. Please God, please, please, please!!!!!!!!!!

July 14th... I don't know what to do!!! I found a note in bed. It was taped to a rock under my pillow. I'm not supposed to tell anyone what I saw. No one! I can't believe it. Why is this happening? Why to Mama? Why to me? God, why won't you answer my prayers??? I stopped wearing makeup. I'm sorry for everything else that I ever did. Please bring my Mama back! I will love you forever. I will even be a missionary. Or a nun—except that we're not Catholic. You know what I mean. PLEASE!!!!!!!!!!

July 17th... I don't understand grownups! I'm supposed to be one soon but I don't understand them at all. I tried talking to Auntie Leah—I wasn't going to tell her everything. But she was too busy cooking dinner. She said Auntie Catherine can't cook because she's too depressed. What about me??? Nobody can talk to Auntie Vonnie. She's too mean! I hate her. Auntie Lizzie has gone back home. Auntie Magdalena (weird, weird, weird!) leaves tomorrow. Their other kids need them back. What about me and Daddy? What do we need? Mama!!!!!!!!!! I hate God! He isn't fair at all!

July 24th... I WANT TO GO HOME!!! Daddy says we can't because Mama might come back anytime. I know she won't. I know it because of what I saw. I wish they'd go. Why are they still here? I promised I wouldn't tell. I wish Harry was here, but he won't answer my letters. I called last night—after every one was in bed, but he wouldn't answer the phone. Maybe his parents wouldn't let him. I know they never liked me. Now they must think I'm crazy. Maybe I am.

July 25th... Susannah doesn't think I'm crazy. Today I almost told her. Thank God I didn't. When I got back to the house there was another note. It was on a rock again. I slept on the floor under my bed. Mama, I am so scared. Mama, I love you.

July 29th... What's the use? I wish I was dead already. Then I wouldn't have to be scared anymore. Then I could see Mama. Oh God, why did you let this happen?

I found Uncle Jonas still in the rocker, his eyes still closed.

"Mr. Weaver?" I whispered He opened his eyes slowly.

"I'm so sorry, Mr. Weaver. All at once this makes it seem so real."

"It's been real to me every day for twenty years."

"Yes, I'm sure. Mr. Weaver, can I please show this to Susannah?"

He said nothing.

"Mr. Weaver, please. My sister needs to see this. She was there when we found Sarah. Please?"

He nodded silently, and I went off to do one of the hardest things I've ever had to do in my life.

I stayed with Susannah until almost supper. Even with the diary to refresh her memory, Susannah could remember very little about that week. If Sarah had divulged any critical information to her, Susannah was unable to retrieve it. What she was able to recover was a whole lot of emotion.

We cried most of the time. Sometimes, oddly, we'd laugh. She'd known Sarah only a short time, but the two of them had bonded in a way that I envied. I envied it then, I envy it now. I told Susannah I loved her, and I knew she would be all right when she told me she loved me back—and then made a face at me.

"Ooh, you're weird," she said, her face streaked with mascara. "All that mushy stuff. You're not—you know?"

"No, and if I was, I wouldn't go for you. You look like a raccoon. A raccoon who ran through Freni's clothesline!"

She hit me with her pillow. I grabbed it away from her and hit her back. Perhaps too hard. At any rate, Shnookums, who'd been napping in her bra, awoke with a yelp.

"Now look what you've done!" Susannah screamed. "That's animal cruelty. I'm going to report you to the SPCA!" She wasn't kidding, bless her.

"Report me, and I'll tell Aaron's aunties what you did with the hand vac last year!"

Her eyes got as big as dinner plates. "How did you know? Magdalena, you wouldn't dare!"

I said I would and left her in a fit of hysterics. Laughter, that is. It would take more than that— maybe a year or two of serious counseling—but my baby sister was going to be all right. I felt like at least one of the weights had been lifted off my chest. Now it was time to get back to the work of finding Sarah's killer. I was going to find whoever it was if it killed me.

15

Magdalena Yoder's Wedding Feast, from Soup to Nuts

Auntie Leah's Pork Chops with Sauerkraut und Apples

4 pork chops
2 tablespoons flour
salt and pepper to taste
3 tablespoons bacon grease
1 large onion (diced)
½ cup brown sugar
2 cups sauerkraut (juice included)
2 apples (peeled, cored, and sliced)
1 tablespoons sesame seeds

Dredge pork chops in flour, and then salt and pepper them. In a heavy skillet brown the chops in bacon grease. Add diced onion and cook a few minutes more. Dissolve brown sugar in kraut juice and return to kraut. Mix in apples and sesame seeds, and spoon over chops. Cover tightly and cook over low heat for 45 minutes.

Serves 4.

16

A promise is a promise. Before supper I made a quick dash into Hernia to see Delores about her rooms. The poor dear must be hard up for entertainment. She laughed so hard she had to turn the volume down on her hearing aid.

"Imagine you coming in personally to see me about a room. If that don't beat all."

"It's for a guest who can't afford my place," I shouted. That should have said it all.

"I could have a fancy place like yours—an inn, you call it. Yes, ma'am, I could have one. All I would have had to do is capitalize on those poor people."

"Those poor people are my people. Why don't you capitalize on your own?"

"Eh?"

I repeated my suggestion, taking great care to enunciate carefully while I stared into her eyes. She took the hint and turned up her hearing aid.

"You don't need to shout, Magdalena."

I smiled amiably. "I wasn't shouting, dear. I was merely making a practical suggestion—from one businesswoman to another. Why not make use of your Methodist connections? You could turn your place into a retreat for other Methodists."

"They already have one."

"Then play up your Methodist heritage and share those quaint qualities with the rest of us. Why, you could call it Wesley World! Now that has a certain ring to it, doesn't it?"

Delores is a mere slip of a woman, all suntanned wrinkles and bottle-blond hair. Her pale eyes look like they might have been bleached as well.

"Methodists aren't in," she said, focusing those colorless corneas accusingly on my countenance.

"We accept converts," I said gaily. "Of course, we are one of the more restrictive denominations. You'd have to give up drinking and dancing for starters."

She grimaced. "So, how long does this guest want to stay? Remember, I'm a rooming house, not a motel. I don't take one-nighters. Too much sheet washing.'

"He wants to stay indefinitely. He's Jonas Weaver. You remember him, don't you?"

"You don't mean Rebecca's husband? The one who went missing?"

I nodded.

"Oh me oh my! If that don't beat everything. I just heard today—it isn't true, is it?"

I was surprised it had taken her so long to hear. Deafness is no barrier to gossip in a town like Hernia. Clearly Norah Hall and her cronies had fallen down on the job.

"It's true," I said.

"In a barrel of apple butter! Imagine that! Well, you tell Jonas he's welcome to come right on over. He can stay as long as he wants. On the house. For old time's sake, tell him."

"Sauerkraut, Delores. Do you know Jonas?"

"Know him? Why, he and I were as sweet as two peas in a pod back in high school. That is, until Rebecca Miller caught his eye."

"Yes. I never paid much attention to her, but from what I've heard, she was beautiful."

"Well, that isn't exactly the word I would have chosen."

"Gorgeous? With bodacious curves?" I couldn't very well use the foul word Sam used, now could I?

Delores smiled, scattering wrinkles in every direction. "Well, now, I don't mean to be unkind, mind you, but she looked rather like you."

"What?"

Delores had the gall to grab one of my hands and pat it. "Face it, Magdalena, you're not exactly a raving beauty. Neither was Rebecca Miller. That's my point. Had she been just another pretty face, Jonas wouldn't have looked twice at her. But, of course, she wasn't. A pretty face, I mean."

"Well, I never!"

"And neither did Rebecca, which is my second point. Women with that kind of disadvantage have that certain special weapon."

"I am not loose!" I snapped.

She raised a penciled eyebrow. "I beg your pardon?"

"When I wear white next Saturday it will be for a good reason."

"Well, that's exactly my point after all."

"It is? From what I hear, Rebecca Miller did more than her share of flirting—and did more than just flirt as well. If you know what I mean."

"Indeed I do, and you are absolutely wrong about that. Rebecca Miller was not a flirt. Pretty girls flirt, dear. Not so pretty girls"—at least she had the decency to look discreetly away—"marry. Some men like that, you know. Girls that will marry them at the drop of a hat. Mama's boys mostly, I'd say."

"My Aaron is not a mama's boy."

"Jonas was, that's for sure. On account of that he couldn't handle a real woman. Not like yours truly. Oh, no, my Jonas had to go and feel sorry for poor homely Becca and marry her." She took a deep breath and peered intently into my eyes. "Is he married now?"

I shrugged. "Not that I can tell."

She patted her dyed do with leathery paws. "You tell poor Jonas he's welcome to stay here as long as he wants."

"I don't think he's looking, dear," I said kindly.

"Nonsense. Every man is looking. They just don't know it."

I tried a different tack. "Well, surely you're not looking. You're one of the pretty ones, remember? You don't have to get married. And Jonas—you said so yourself—is just a mama's boy."

"Well, that was then, and this is now," she said, sounding just like Susannah.

It was my turn to grab one of her hands. "Look, Toots, Jonas Weaver is off limits. His daughter is being buried this week, for heaven's sake. Besides which, he is still a Mennonite. A Mennonite, not a Methodist." I didn't mean to hiss that final word.

The pale pupils peered peevishly at me. "Why, Magdalena Yoder, I don't believe it. You're jealous! You're getting married Saturday to Hernia's most eligible bachelor, but you still want Jonas on the side!"

"That's an ugly lie!" I screamed and exited quickly, with most of my dignity still intact.

And indeed it was a lie. Aaron Miller Jr. was all the man I would ever need. Perhaps even more. I certainly didn't need a man Jonas's age on the side. It just irritated me that some women—my baby sister included—have got to get their claws into every available man who passes within striking distance. It was bad enough that Susannah did it, but in Delores's case it was ridiculous, if not downright obscene. The woman was old enough to be a great-grandmother, no less, and here she was, slinking around like a vamp.

It had to be sex that was to blame. Carnal knowledge was the downfall of Adam and Eve and has been the downfall of every generation since. It is all some people seem to think about. The human loins— to use one of Mama's favorite words—appear to be the strongest motivational force on the planet. People are nothing but mere puppets, controlled by pubic pulses. Mama, you were right. "Loin" is a four-letter word!

But I didn't get it. Not yet, at any rate. Come Saturday night, however, and the mystery of life might well be revealed to me. A shudder of delicious anticipation ran through me, and for a split second I forgot to feel guilty.

When I got back to the inn I found Freni in a huff. This, of course, was nothing new, but it was nothing to sneeze at either. If Freni quit on me, I'd have to feed that crowd myself, or recruit Auntie Leah. But, given the fact that I was about to stab Auntie Leah in the back (figuratively, I assure you), I didn't feel right about pressing her into service as my chef, no matter how willing she seemed.

"What's wrong, dear?" I asked with practiced sympathy.

"It's that Leah woman," she snapped. "Always popping into my kitchen and giving advice where it's not needed."

I maturely refrained from reminding Freni that it was really my kitchen and that she might actually be able to benefit from some of Leah's advice.

"Just consider the source," I said, quoting Mama.

"Ach, but if that source sticks her head in here one more time, I quit!"

"Freni, dear, you wouldn't want to deprive these people of another opportunity to rave about your scrumptious cooking, would you?"

She waved a blue enamel ladle at me. "Flattery will get you nowhere, Magdalena."

"But they are all from out of town, dear. When they get back home they won't stop talking about what a wonderful cook you are. You'll be famous."

For a mere second or two a dreamy look swept over her face. Then it was gone. She put down the ladle.

"Pride is a sin, Magdalena. Shame on you for trying to tempt me. Besides, all your guests are from out of town. I'm probably already famous and just don't know it."

"I'm sure you are, dear. But those other guests are all English. These guests are Mennonite. When these guests go back, your fame will spread throughout the Mennonite and Amish communities. 'Freni Hostetler' will become a household word among the plain people."

"Get behind me, Satan!" she said, but her eyes had glazed over.

I knew I had Freni just where I wanted her, and I was about to sew things up with one last compliment when the source did indeed stick her head back into the kitchen.

"How are things coming in here?" Leah boomed.

Freni looked like Lot's wife turned into a pillar of salt. "Magdalena," she grunted through gritted teeth.

"Leah!"

I raced to head her off. But despite her great size, the woman could indeed move like a freight train. By the time I reached her, she had breached Freni's holy of holies and was peering into the oven.

"That pork roast looks a little dry," she said. "You might want to add a little water and tent it with aluminum foil."

Without another word Freni threw down her apron, and without another word Auntie Leah picked it up and put it on. Of course it didn't fit, but that mattered naught. The mantle of chef had been passed, albeit unpleasantly, and Auntie Leah knew a trophy when she saw one.

Perhaps I should have run after my cousin, pleading with her on bended knee to come back. But I was tired, and Freni, I knew without a doubt, would reappear bright and early the next morning. There would be plenty of time to eat crow then.

"When did you say supper was?" Leah demanded.

"Six. Will the roast be done in time?"

Leah's laugh is more curious than it is unpleasant. It is reminiscent of the fireworks they shoot over in Bedford on the Fourth of July, but without the bright colors, of course.

"Done?" she finally rasped. "Five more minutes and we could chop this thing into charcoal briquettes."

"But Aaron and his father are joining us tonight," I wailed.

"Not to worry. Tell everyone that supper has been postponed until seven and promise them a meal they won't forget."

I did what I was told, little realizing that the promise could come true in more ways than one.

The entire herd, along with their cowboys, assembled for supper, so along with Jonas, Susannah, and the two Aarons, we had a full house. True to her word, Auntie Leah had managed to turn a sow's ear into a silk purse. Well, not literally, of course. But she had managed to turn the dried-out pork roast into something she called barbecue.

"It's Southern," she explained, almost loud enough to break the sound barrier. "Sol and I took a trip down south last year. We stopped at a place called Bubba's Carolina Barbecue and they served us this."

"South Carolina has some wonderful golf courses, and big-bass fishing—"

"Can the travelogue, Sol," Auntie Vonnie snapped. She looked at me accusingly. "You said supper would be something special. I was expecting at least a nice prime rib. This looks like shredded pork in sauce."

"It is. You eat it on a bun, like Sloppy Joes. The sauce is different, though. It's something special. I made it myself from a recipe I brought back with me."

"It's good," Auntie Lizzie declared, and I breathed a sigh of relief.

If it was good enough for Auntie Lizzie, who had class, then it was good enough for the rest of us. Besides, in addition to the barbecue, there was enough Swiss-German hot potato salad on the table to feed an army. With the fresh sweet peas, homemade applesauce, and shoofly pie for dessert, no Mennonite worth the heritage was going to go hungry.

"Putrid, pupa, puke," Susannah mumbled.

I kicked her deftly under the table. I'm sure my sister didn't mean to be rude. A generous person would call her behaviorally challenged.

It was clear from the way folks had arranged themselves at the table that a battle was brewing. A very lopsided battle, if you ask me. The Beeftrust and their herders, including Aaron Senior, were keeping themselves as far away from the bereaved father as possible. Susannah sat to my immediate left, Aaron Junior to my right. As a gesture of respect, and as a means of extending my condolences, I had placed Uncle Jonas at the end of the table opposite me. The Beeftrust, however, were leaning heavily toward my end of the table, like corpulent palms caught in a hurricane. Either they felt that death was contagious or they had it in for the poor man. Given what I already knew of them, it was a toss-up.

"So, Uncle Jonas, how was your flight?" I asked for everyone's benefit.

My Pooky Bear beamed at my diplomacy skills.

"Bumpy," Uncle Jonas said. He looked like he was about to bolt.

"Was it? I've never flown, you know. I'd love to, of course. I've just never had the opportunity. Mama never saw the sense in it, and then after she died—well, I've just been too busy."

"Travel isn't what it's cracked up to be," Auntie Vonnie said, her mouth full of bun. "We went to Europe last summer, and it was boring. If you've seen one museum, you've seen them all, if you ask me. Did you know they actually put broken statues in them?"

"Really?"

"With no arms and legs! Some of them don't even have heads. It must be their economy, Rudy says. All this talk about how weak our dollar is and how strong their currencies are— well, it's all stuff and nonsense. Just look at their museums."

"You don't say!"

"Oh, yes. But I will admit that the little foot baths they put in all the hotel rooms are mighty soothing after walking on those cobblestones all day."

"Well, I've always enjoyed traveling," Auntie Lizzie said sweetly. "Manasses and I keep talking about a trip to the Holy Land. Where would you go, dear, if you had the chance?"

I graced her with a warm smile. "Well, I'm not sure. I'd have—" I was reaching to pass the platter of barbecue buns when I noticed the word "Japan" stenciled on the bottom. "Japan," I said quickly.

Auntie Lizzie nodded approvingly. "Good choice. That's where I'd go. After the Holy Land, of course. These days Asia is a much more chic destination than Europe. And Japan, I hear, is the place to be."

"Definitely," Uncle Jonas said.

"Moo goo gai pan," Auntie Magdalena whimpered.

"No, that's Chinese, dear," I informed her kindly.

"She said, 'You knew Diane.' She said it to him." Uncle Elias, having translated his wife's garbled verbiage, nodded in the direction of Uncle Jonas.

"Who is Diane?" I asked politely.

"Diane Lefcourt, a friend of Becca's," Leah boomed. "As far as anyone knows, she was the last person to speak to our sister—besides you-know-who."

"Really?" I presumed that the you-know-who in question was the murderer, not Uncle Jonas.

Uncle Jonas squirmed. "Of course I knew Diane. She was my wife's best friend, damn it!"

"You know what she means," Uncle Elias said. "You knew that Diane was a bad influence on Becca."

"Amen," Aaron Senior said.

"Amen," everyone chorused, except for Susannah, younger Aaron, and me.

"My Becca was a grown woman, and I didn't pick her friends," Uncle Jonas growled.

"Birds of a feather flock together," Auntie Lizzie said primly. "And there was always trouble following that Diane woman."

"Ah, yes, that Diane woman," Uncle Rudy said, sounding wistful. We all looked at him and he shrugged.

"Did you tell her?" Uncle Jonas said suddenly to me.

"I didn't even know this Diane person, dear."

He gave me a knowing look. "Not that. I'm talking about Leah and my condition."

"What condition?" Auntie Leah sat bolt upright in her seat. "And what's it have to do with me?"

"Mucus, membrane, melanin," Susannah mumbled. I kicked her sharply again. She was acting strange even for herself.

"Well?" Auntie Leah demanded.

"Nothing dear," I said quickly. "She's just talking gibberish."

"Not her—him!"

"A deal's a deal," Uncle Jonas said calmly. "If you don't tell her, then I will."

"Tell me what?" Lacking a proper neck, Auntie Leah had to turn her torso to look at Uncle Jonas. All of us, Susannah included, stared in the direction indicated.

"Oh, it's just something about a diary," I said casually. "I'll tell you after supper."

"Diary?" my sister asked.

I patted her arm. "You know, Susannah, Sarah's diary."

All faces turned my way.

I took a deep breath. When the cat is out of the bag already, you have only two choices as far as I can see: pretend you let the cat out on purpose or put the bag over your head and hope you suffocate. I wasn't about to do the latter, not with Pooky Bear about to be mine. I mean truly mine.

"Uncle Jonas has Sarah's diary. In it Sarah mentions that she knows who killed her mother. Jonas and I thought it would be a great idea if we showed it to the police. Don't you all agree?"

There was a chorus of "yes's." In retrospect there weren't as many "yes's" as I might have expected, but I was too distracted by that damn cat to notice who abstained.

"It isn't yours to show," Uncle Jonas said quietly.

Nine heads and one torso swiveled to face the opposite end of the table.

"Well, she was my niece," Leah boomed.

"Here, here," someone said.

"Ah, you," Uncle Jonas said accusingly to Leah.

"Me what? Out with it, Jonas! What is it you're accusing me of this time?"

He sat there like a tidy little Buddha, smiling placidly, his hands folded in his lap. "Magdalena?" he said at last, his voice as scratchy as Mama's old phonograph records of gospel music. "You care to do the honors, or shall I?"

I took a deep breath. My hands were balled into fists, something that genetics all but prevents me from doing. Clearly I was not a willing partner in this crime.

"Uncle Jonas would prefer that it be a private burial," I said quickly, "with none of us present."

"Impossible!"

"Unheard of!"

"Absolutely not!"

"That's ridiculous!"

"No way!"

The last was from Susannah. I patted her reassuringly.

"Well, how about limited attendance at the funeral?" I felt like Abraham arguing with God over the fate of doomed Sodom and Gomorrah.

"What do you mean, limited attendance?" My very own Pooky Bear was the first to challenge me.

"Well, it has been twenty years, hasn't it? I mean, we don't all need to attend, do we? Suppose just some of us went and the others stayed home?"

"Why?" Auntie Lizzie was now betraying me.

"Why? Well, uh—well, suppose Uncle Jonas didn't want all of us there?" It was a mere whisper.

All eyes shifted to Uncle Jonas again, but he only smiled and nodded at me, so they whipped their heads around yet again. They were like observers of a miniature tennis match— all except poor Auntie Leah, of course, who had to swivel her torso. Undoubtedly the woman has a flat, tight tummy that belies her girth.

I looked past her and fixed my gaze on a spot on Uncle Sol's collar. "Okay, Uncle Jonas doesn't want one of you in particular to be there. If you will all see me privately after supper, I'll let you know if it's you, in which case you will have time to come up with a decent excuse of your own to stay away and nobody will need to get hurt." There, do I sound like a mean-spirited woman?

"Why is this mystery person being banned from the funeral in the first place?" Auntie Leah bellowed.

"Let's just say—"

Uncle Jonas put a hand straight out in front of him, palm out, as if to stop me physically. "Because my Sarah asked this mystery person for help, and they turned her away."

Auntie Leah gasped. "That's awful!"

"Then why did you do it?" Uncle Jonas asked softly.

17

"What?" The townsfolk were going to accuse the YY air force of sonic booms again.

"I am accusing you of turning your back on my daughter when she needed you. She went to you, Leah, after her mother's death, to tell you what she saw, but you turned her away."

"I did no such thing!"

"Apparently you were too busy. And she was just a kid. A kid who ended up dying because of you."

"That's unfair," Auntie Lizzie cried, and we all voiced our agreement.

"It's in the diary. You read it, Magdalena."

"I dig pot," Auntie Magdalena whimpered.

"She did not," Uncle Elias translated quickly.

Everyone looked at me.

"Sarah didn't word it nearly that strong," I said gently. "Anyway, how were you to know what she wanted to tell you?"

"Never turn a child away," Auntie Vonnie humphed. "Jesus himself gave us that example in the Bible."

"He certainly did." Uncle Rudy patted his wife's wrist, the perfect example of a supportive husband.

Auntie Vonnie ran with the encouragement. "I'd have to say I see poor Jonas's point of view quite clearly. If he wants a private burial, then so be it."

Uncle Rudy nodded.

"It's all right with me," Uncle Manasses said, much to my surprise. "Jonas is her father, after all. He should have his say." He turned to Aunt Lizzie. "What do you think, dear?"

"Well, well, well" was all Auntie Lizzie said, but somewhere in the distance I heard a cock crow three times.

I was shocked at the way the room had polarized into two camps. Or at least I assumed it had. But perhaps I was wrong and everyone had turned against poor Auntie Leah. And if that was indeed the case, would I be brave enough to stand up for her?

"Auntie Magdalena, what about you? What do you have to say?"

"Leroy has a cart of mould," she moaned.

"She said Leah has a heart of gold," Uncle Elias said crisply. "And I agree."

Auntie Magdalena mumbled a few more things and Elias nodded vigorously. When she was done he looked around the room slowly, his gaze settling briefly on each married couple.

"It is damn easy to get distracted when you're a parent. There were any number of times when my own kids have tried to talk to me, but I was too busy just then. It's happened to everyone. So, even though we haven't seen the diary, my wife and I feel that it should have no bearing on whether or not Leah gets to attend the funeral. The funeral is, after all, a family event, and Leah is family."

"But you're not," Vonnie said.

Mine wasn't the only gasp.

"What's that supposed to mean?" Elias's dark eyes flashed.

"I simply meant that this is a decision that should be made by blood."

"Blood, bile, boogers," Susannah intoned.

Auntie Vonnie gave Susannah a withering look and linked her arm through Uncle Rudy's. "And anyway, what Elias just said doesn't apply to us. We always had time to listen to our kids. And our neighbors' kids as well. Had young Sarah come to me with her problem, she'd be sitting here today."

"Aaron?" I looked beseechingly at my beloved.

My Pooky Bear cleared his throat. "I'd kind of like to take a peek into the diary first. Leah, at the very least, should get a chance to see what it says. In this country we're innocent until proven guilty."

I patted Aaron's arm discreetly. "Pops?"

Aaron Senior swallowed an enormous bite of hot potato salad. Our discussion had not slowed down his ingestion process in the least. "Judge not, that ye be not judged," he said carefully. "At least I think that's how it goes. Damn, but I wish I still had my King James version."

"Susannah?"

"Gall, gook, gangrene."

"Susannah!"

"What?" The look she gave me was devoid of deceit, and I felt my stomach do a flip. Tomorrow I was going to have to trot out the yellow pages and look up a therapist over in Bedford. I had been sadly mistaken about her recovery.

"Hey, you didn't ask me," Uncle Sol said.

As we turned to look at him, Auntie Leah looked away. Possibly she had reason to believe her own husband would betray her.

"What about it, Uncle Sol?" I asked calmly. "Do you think Uncle Jonas has the right to bar an aunt from attending her niece's funeral?"

Uncle Sol stood up. Given the uncles' height it is sometimes hard to tell if they're standing or sitting, but I saw the napkin fall from his lap.

"Leah and I have been partners now for fifty-two years. I stand by my wife. Leah should definitely get to read that diary, but regardless of what it says, she's going to that funeral. She and Sarah were very close." He sat down again, disappearing briefly while he recovered his napkin.

"Well, there you go," I said to Uncle Jonas. "That's eight against five. It seems pretty clear what the majority has ruled."

Uncle Jonas gave us one of his neat smiles. Then he began to speak in that voice that can put new grooves in your records.

"This is absolutely absurd. First of all, she"—he pointed to Susannah—"isn't even part of the family. Besides which, she didn't express a valid opinion. She should be locked up, if you ask me."

"Nobody asked you," I snapped.

"And the Miller men both equivocated. As for you, Miss Magdalena Yoder—you aren't part of the family either."

I linked arms with my Pooky Bear. "I will be, come Saturday."

Had I not been a pacifist and seated at the opposite end of the table, I would have knocked that tidy smile off his face. "Well, now," he said, "while you were all out gallivanting today, I made a few calls. I even spoke to this Melvin person. My little Sarah's funeral is going to be Wednesday afternoon at three o'clock, Beechy Grove Mennonite Church. You are all invited except for Leah."

Twelve pairs of eyes stared, twelve mouths hung open. I was the first to recover.

"Get out of my house, Jonas Weaver! You are no longer welcome here. Delores Brown has a room waiting for you on Maple Street. She takes all kinds."

I, however, was the first one to get up from the table. I can't stand for folks to see me cry.

A scratchy roar may not be as bloodcurdling as a high-pitched scream, but it will get your attention. When it persisted too long to be merely a stubbed toe or a whacked crazy bone, we gathered, one by one, in the hall outside Uncle Jonas's room.

"It was right here in my suitcase!"

I pushed through the throng. "What was? The diary?"

"No shit, Sherlock. What else?"

I said a silent prayer that the ghost of Grandma Yoder would continue to sleep peacefully. This had been her room, after all, and the only four-letter word my Pennsylvania Dutch-speaking grandmother knew was "soap," something she fed me liberal amounts of when I tried to teach her more.

"Are you sure it's missing?" someone asked.

Uncle Jonas pointed to the contents of his suitcase, spread across the bed in the neatest little piles you could imagine. Every item of clothing was folded just so. Even his socks—which had clearly been ironed—were folded, edge to edge, not balled, like Mama used to do with Daddy's. His toiletries were lined up in precise rows, like soldiers on parade. There was obviously no diary.

"Maybe you misplaced it somewhere else," I suggested helpfully.

He glared at me. "I loaned the book to you."

"Yes, you're quite right. But then I gave it back, remember? Just before I ran into town to see Delores."

"You gave it back, all right, but you stood there and watched while I returned it to my suitcase. You knew exactly where it was."

"Your suitcase has a lock, doesn't it? Why didn't you lock it?"

"I did. Obviously you found out the combination somehow."

I felt my Aaron lay a restraining hand on my shoulder, but I shrugged it off. "I did no such thing. This is absolute nonsense. Why on earth would I want to steal your diary when I'd already read it?"

He had the nerve to give me that tidy smile again. "You were the only one who knew about it, Miss Yoder."

I started to take a step forward, but the pressure of Aaron's hand increased. "Yes, I was the only one who knew about it until supper. Then everyone knew." Blinded by rage, I trampled right over my family-to-be's feelings. "Why, with this bunch, I wouldn't be surprised if the king of Siam knew by now."

"That's Thailand," he said.

'What?"

"Siam is Thailand now. Has been since 1939."

"You know what I mean, buster. Besides, Melvin Stoltzfus, our chief of police, knows about it."

He pointed a manicured finger at me. "You told him already?"

"I was laying groundwork, Uncle Jonas. Anyway, you can be sure that Melvin didn't sneak in and swipe it. He's not that bright. Poor man once tried to milk a bull."

He blinked. "That man is your police chief? The one you wanted me to show my Sarah's diary to? The one I spoke to this afternoon?"

"Hey, I was upfront with you. I told you his name when I called you in Florida."

"I haven't even been back to visit here for twenty years. How the hell was I supposed to remember a name? But the bull-milking, that I remember. That was back when we were still living here. Everyone was saying he should have been jailed for animal cruelty."

"He was kicked in the head," I said. "That was punishment enough."

Even his grunts were raspy. "Look, all I know is you were the first one to leave the table tonight. You could have come straight on up here and stolen the diary. In fact, I'd bet my life you did."

What with his swearing and betting, it was clear that life in Sarasota, despite its large Mennonite and Amish communities, had led Uncle Jonas a ways from the fold. It wouldn't surprise me if he'd secretly converted to Presbyterianism along the way.

"No, you look," I said, trying to ignore Aaron's fingers digging into my back. "I'm the one who went to the trouble of looking you up. For reasons that have become apparent, none of the others—even your so-called allies—could be bothered. I sent my fiancé all the way over to Pittsburgh to get you, I put you up in my inn, I went to town and found you term lodgings, and now you have the nerve to treat me like this? Well, I won't have it."

I wiggled out of Aaron's grasp, pushed Uncle Jonas aside, and proceeded to pack his suitcase for him. I did not pack his suitcase the way he would have liked. When I was done it looked like Susannah's bag would look at the end of one of her escapades, if Susannah used luggage.

"You get out of my inn, Jonas Weaver." I turned to the others. "And any of you others who want to try and stop

Auntie Leah from attending her own niece's funeral can do the same. This is supposed to be a family I'm marrying into, not a herd of stampeding cattle."

The bovine imagery was unintentional, but it didn't seem to offend anyone. There was a smattering of applause, and no one but Jonas Weaver left the premises.

I have never been entranced by watching fires, but stargazing is another thing. I can gaze at a summer sky for hours. At the PennDutch we are just far enough removed from the lights of Hernia to see some spectacular nighttime skies, and that night was a doozy. All the queen's diamonds, spread across a bolt of dusty blue velvet, could not have been more impressive.

When I was twelve I saved up my allowance and bought a cheap telescope at a secondhand store over in Bedford. Along with it came a tattered book on astronomy. That summer was one of the happiest in my life, although—and I am ashamed to admit it—my new hobby turned me into a sinner faster that Eve could swallow that apple.

Every night when the sky was clear, I would sneak out after my bedtime and study the stars for hours. Disobeying one's parents is a sin, and like the Bible says, sin has a way of getting found out. It wasn't long before Mama noticed the dark circles under my eyes and accused me of you-know-what. Unfortunately I didn't know what you-know-what was then, and in an effort to shorten the lecture, I made a full confession.

"You caught me," I said. "I do it every night. I could do it for hours at a time. Mama, I wish you and Papa would try it. I just know you would love it."

That was the day I ate a whole bar of Camay soap.

Once when Susannah was little I tried to explain the constellations to her.

"That's Ursa Major, the Big Dipper," I said.

"It looks leaky."

"And that's Virgo, the virgin."

"Are you a virgin, Magdalena?"

"Over there is Taurus, the bull."

"You can say that again."

I gave up.

Even when they found out what I was really up to, my parents did not share my fascination with the heavens. It confused them too much. That mankind should inhabit a minuscule planet in such a vast universe did not make sense to them. Anyway, it was heaven with a capital H that interested them. In the end I decided that stargazing was best enjoyed as a solitary pursuit (much like you-know-what, or so I've been told).

I was sitting on a rocker looking up at Canes Venatici with my naked eye when I felt Aaron's now-familiar touch on my shoulder.

"Beautiful," he murmured.

"Wait until everyone's asleep and all the lights are off," I said.

"Why, Magdalena, what a surprise!"

"I was talking about the stars, Aaron!"

"But I was talking about you." He squatted down on one haunch and laid his head on my shoulder. I could feel his long, dark lashes flickering against my cheek.

I held my breath, willing time to stop. Of course it didn't, and when I exhaled I sounded like a disgruntled horse.

"I love you, Magdalena Yoder, you know that?"

"Yes." I was dying to say "I love you too," but it is so hard for me to say the L word. I always require a mental rehearsal first.

"I was proud of you tonight, Magdalena."

"Thank you." I could have kicked myself for leaving off the "dear." If I can say "dear" to strangers, why can't I say it to the man I love?

"You make me the happiest man in the whole wide world," my Pooky Bear said.

"I have a telescope somewhere up in the attic," I heard myself say. "I'd really like to show you Uranus."

It was the most romantic thing I could think of to say.

18

Sure enough, when I stumbled into the kitchen the next morning, there was Freni, bustling about as usual. She was even whistling a happy time, but she stopped abruptly when she heard me come in.

"Freni," I said brightly. "You have a nice walk?" Freni lives directly behind me and actually prefers to walk through the woods rather than to come by any sort of conveyance. That is not a religious preference, mind you, but one based firmly on stubbornness.

She turned, spatula in hand, and stared at me. "I'm eighty years old, Magdalena. I'm lucky I can walk at all."

"You're seventy-four, Freni."

"Close enough. Are those English going to sleep all day?"

"They're Mennonites," I reminded her for the umpteenth time, "and they're not on any sort of schedule. Maybe we could make breakfast a help-yourself situation. You know, put out a couple of boxes of cereal, some juice, the toaster and a loaf of bread."

"Ach! What kind of a breakfast is that?" Freni squawked. "I've got bacon and eggs here that need to be used before the end of the week."

"Well, I hate to see you tied to the stove all morning. What if we invite those who want a hot breakfast to make their own?"

Will I ever learn? Despite her temper, Freni doesn't have a violent bone in her body. Still, that spatula came perilously close to my ears. Both of them. A deaf person, watching her from behind, might have concluded that she was trying to conduct a one-person orchestra.

"They come in, I go out." Freni was mad enough to lapse into Pennsylvania Dutch, her mother tongue. "Is that clear, Magdalena?"

"Yah." I can't speak Deutsche, but I can understand it. Chances are I could understand Freni if she was speaking Chinese.

"Now you go right on upstairs and wake them all up. Tell them that I'm making pancakes, sausage, and bacon, and I want to know how they want their eggs. Tell them they eat in thirty minutes."

"Yah. Quite clear," I said respectfully. "But before I go I want to ask a question."

"What happened last night between my daughter- in-law and myself is none of your business," she said. She was speaking English again.

That anything had happened between Barbara and Freni was news to me, but I resisted the temptation to pry. It took a tremendous amount of strength on my part, and the fingernail marks on my palms may well stay with me the rest of my life.

"It's not about that, dear. Do you know a woman named Diane Lefcourt?"

The way Freni clucked, I wouldn't have been surprised if she had personally supplied our breakfast eggs.

"Ach, Magdalena, whatever made you think of her?"

"They talked about her at dinner last night. Someone said she was a bad influence on Aaron's aunt Rebecca."

Freni's spatula waved the orchestra into a loud crescendo. "That Diane woman was a bad influence on the devil himself. All of Hernia breathed a sigh of relief when she ran off with that mattress salesman from Johnstown."

"Johnstown, Pennsylvania?"

"Ach, what other Johnstown is there? Now go wake up the English, Magdalena. The sausages will get tough if they sit too long, and a cold pancake is fit only for pigs."

I scurried off to do her bidding, visions of the over-done pork roast supplying unexpected energy. It was not, of course, a pleasant task. My rooms do not possess Do Not Disturb signs.

"Go away," someone in Auntie Vonnie's room grunted.

'Two eggs basted easy, two eggs over medium," Auntie Leah boomed.

"More lies, you're queasy," Auntie Magdalena moaned.

I briefly protested my innocence, and then to be on the safe side, jotted down "Four fried, over easy."

From Auntie Lizzie's room there was no answer. There were sounds to be heard, however, and I grimly resolved to oil those bedsprings before assigning that room again. In the daytime, and at their age!

"Breakfast is in thirty minutes," I called to my sister.

Susannah didn't answer either, and, as usual, her door was locked.

"Look, you sleepyhead," I said, "you better get up this instant, or else." Actually, one might possibly have interpreted it as yelling, but my doors are thick and Susannah is a sound sleeper. At any rate, I got no response.

I pounded briefly on the door. "If I have to put up with this bunch, so do you. In fact, if you're the last one downstairs, then you can just kiss my hospitality goodbye. The day has finally come when you're going to get a job, Susannah. Do you hear me? A real job. Then you can pay me rent!"

Feeling self-righteous, albeit justifiably so, I went downstairs and gave Freni the orders. I told her to scramble Susannah's eggs. I told her Auntie Lizzie and Uncle Manasses wanted theirs poached—in Tabasco sauce.

"Ach!" Freni said, shaking her head, but then she did what she was told. To her, there is no explaining the English and their funny ways.

Everyone showed up at breakfast on time except Susannah. I swallowed my irritation and strove to be the best hostess I knew how to be.

"So," I said brightly, "what have we planned for today? Another picnic, perhaps? Aaron and I discovered this really lovely spot by a stream over on Evitt's Mountain. I'd be happy to give you directions."

There were no takers.

"Well, then, I hear the library in Bedford is hosting a show on miniatures. You know, these teeny-weeny rooms all decorated with the tiniest—"

"We're not interested," Auntie Vonnie snapped.

"Well, maybe I am," Auntie Magdalena said with surprising clarity.

"Me too," Auntie Leah boomed.

"Provincial," Auntie Lizzie sniffed. And to think I had looked up to her.

I realized suddenly that my guests had polarized themselves in their seating choices as well. Auntie Leah and her supporters were on my left, Uncle Jonas's supporters to my right. It was like Judgment Day, only the two sides were reversed as far as I was concerned, and I was certainly in no position to play God.

However, I was not averse to playing Mama. After all, if my Pooky Bear was so bent on us having a family, I was going to need all the practice I could muster, and Susannah knew me too well to be a cooperative pupil.

"Well, that settles it," I said, my voice still gay. "We'll play Amish today."

"Just what, pray tell, is that?" Auntie Lizzie asked. The Tabasco sauce hadn't seemed to faze either her or Uncle Manasses.

I smiled. "Oh, playing Amish can be loads of fun, dear. You and Auntie Leah will take down the drapes in the den and—"

"I'll do no such thing," Auntie Leah bellowed.

"But you will," I said calmly. "You'll all do the chores I assign you, or you can find accommodations elsewhere. Of course, you'd owe me for the nights you've already spent here."

Uncle Rudy slapped his wallet on the table. "I'll pay you for the damned nights. How much is it?"

I chuckled pleasantly. "This is a very expensive establishment, you know. Celebrities come here from all over the world to savor the ambience, and ambience doesn't come cheap."

Uncle Rudy waved a fistful of hundred-dollar bills. "Quit beating around the bush, Yoder, and tell me what the damages are."

I politely refrained from laughing. "And unfortunately, June is my high season. Still, you are Aaron's family, so I've decided to give you a ten percent discount. No, make that a twenty percent discount, on account of you'll all be my family too come Saturday."

Uncle Rudy smirked and tucked all but one of the hundreds back in his wallet.

I pulled one of my inn's brochures out of my dress pocket and did some quick mental arithmetic. "Okay, that will be sixteen twenty per couple. I've rounded it off so it includes tax."

Everyone laughed—at my expense, I might add. Uncle Rudy flung me the hundred-dollar bill.

"I'm afraid you misunderstood me," I said gently.

Uncle Rudy's mocking eyes were mere slits. "So, I'm feeling generous today. I'll pay for them too."

I prayed for patience. "Is this a joke? I said sixteen twenty, and this is a hundred-dollar bill."

"Keep the change."

I leaned over the table and spread the brochure out between them. "That was sixteen hundred and twenty dollars, dears."

"Why, that's highway robbery," Auntie Magdalena said, clear as a bell.

I smiled benevolently, like a good mother. "My New York and L.A. customers don't seem to think so. Ivana tells me it's cheap. And the Spielbergs— generous tippers to a fault."

"Well, I'm not tipping you a damn thing," Uncle Rudy shouted. "Hell, if I'm going to pay at all."

"Such language from a Mennonite!" I chided him gently. "Well, then, I guess you've decided to play Amish for the day."

Without further ado I assigned them all chores that I'd been putting off for some time. Of course they complained bitterly, but I ignored them, just like Mama used to ignore me. As they trotted reluctantly off after breakfast, I nabbed Uncle Elias.

"I don't suppose you're wondering why I assigned you to help Mose clean out the cow stalls."

He glared at me. "No."

"I'll tell you anyway," I said charitably. "It has to do with your shoes."

"My shoes?" He glanced down at a pair of those elaborate, state-of-the-art running shoes, the kind that do everything but move your feet for you.

"Yeah, your shoes. You already stepped in a cow pie this morning, dear, so I didn't think you'd mind."

"I don't know what you're talking about."

"Can the innocent act," I said. "Attached to this face is a genuine Yoder nose. I can smell a mouse pass gas at the other end of the house. Cow pie on your shoes is a breeze. Not literally, of course."

Uncle Elias braced himself against a chair and displayed the sole of his right shoe. "I cleaned it off as best I could. Even rubbed aftershave into the tread."

"I know, and your brand is passe," I said kindly. "You should ask Aaron what he uses. At any rate, what I really want to know is, what were you doing over on Aaron's farm so early this morning? Sleepwalking?"

Uncle Elias crossed his arms. "Who says I was walking on his farm? You have cows, don't you?"

"Don't even try to fool this nose, dear," I said patiently. "The Millers just field-graze their cows this time of the year, but I give mine alfalfa pellets on the side. Different diets, different odors."

He stared at me. "You're kidding, right?"'

"Dead serious."

Actually, I was full of baloney—about the different odors, I mean. I knew, however, that Uncle Elias had not been tramping through my small pasture. I have only two cows, but they are surprisingly antisocial. When anyone other than Mose or myself gets within fifty feet of them, they bellow louder than

Auntie Leah. I preferred that Uncle Elias believe in the powers of my schnoz, though, over a more simple, logical explanation. Something didn't smell quite right about that man, and it wasn't just his shoe.

"So, I woke up early and couldn't go back to sleep. So I took a little walk on my brother-in-law's farm. So what?"

"You dig up the floor of the root cellar?" I asked calmly.

His mouth opened so wide I could see the stains on his back molars. I would get Freni to recommend a good denture paste.

"Well, Uncle Elias, did you find anything interesting?"

"Not a thing!" he said at last. "The dirt in there is packed hard as a brick."

"Hmm. You try the barn?"

He looked sheepish. "Didn't have time. You farm folks get up mighty early. Young Aaron almost caught me as it was. And it didn't help that I stepped on a cat."

"Instead of going early, go late," I suggested sensibly. "We farm folks start nodding off as early as nine. After midnight it's only the devil by himself."

"Gotcha," he said, his eyes twinkling. "I'll be sure and tell you what I find."

"You better," I said, with mock sternness. "And walk up the driveway next time. That pasture can be treacherous in the dark."

We both laughed.

It was a simple matter to call directory assistance for Johnstown. They did indeed have a Lefcourt listed, but only one, and the first name was Samuel. I called anyway. Nowadays nothing surprises me.

"Mr. Samuel Lefcourt?"

"Yes." He sounded as if I had awakened him.

"You didn't perchance used to be Diane Lefcourt?"

"What?"

"It's all right if you were. I mean, I'm used to the Hollywood crowd and—"

"My mother was Diane Lefcourt."

My heart sank. "She was? You mean she's already passed on?"

"Who the hell are you?" Samuel said, now obviously wide awake.

"An old acquaintance," I said quickly. It wasn't really a lie. After all, I lived right across the road from the Miller farm. It's quite possible I had met Diane that fateful summer when she stopped by my neighbors' to visit Rebecca.

"You a goddamn bill collector?" Samuel asked. I heard giggling in the background.

"To the contrary, dear. There may even be a little money coming to Diane. If she's still alive."

"You can send it me," Samuel said. The giggling got louder.

"No, this is something she has to sign. She is still alive, then, I take it?"

"Yeah," Samuel said grudgingly. "She's still alive. I don't know her number, but you'll find her in the Bedford phone book. Look under convents. Something about a broken heart. Oh, and her name isn't Diane anymore."

"It's not?"

"It's Sister Angelica. Can you dig it?"

I had just put the phone back in its cradle when Susannah came bursting into my room. I have been training her not to do that for thirty-four years, but to no avail. If my sister were a dog, she would make her pet Shnookums seem brilliant by comparison.

"Susannah! Knock first!"

"Oh, Mags, I don't have time for that. I got it!"

"You've seen the light? You want to be a Mennonite again?"

"Very funny! I've got a job, that's what!"

"You mean my yelling at you this morning did some good?"

"What are you talking about, Mags? I left the house this morning before you even got up."

"What?"

"Well, I wanted to be the first one to apply. Just in case there were oodles of applicants,, you know. And there were. But at ten-fifty an hour, can you blame them?"

"Burger Bucket pays that high?"

My baby sister gathered her swirls and pirouetted proudly around the room. "I won't be working for Burger Bucket, sister dearest. I am now the official paint namer for Crazy Paints, Inc."

"What?"

"There were sixty-five applicants, you know. But none of the others were as fast on their feet thinking up names. Go ahead, pick a letter. Any letter."

"A letter?"

"Of the alphabet, silly. Like S, for instance."

"Okay, S.".

"That's easy. Slime, sewage, slobber."

"Those are colors' names?"

"They are now. Crazy Paints Incorporated is the company with the vision necessary to take us into the twenty-first century."

"When everyone will be color-blind, I hope. So that's what you were doing last night at the table? Making up names for colors?"

Susannah beamed. "And I'm good, aren't I? Go ahead and name another letter, sis."

"Q," I said, perhaps meanly.

"Quagmire, quartan, quahog," she said smoothly.

She was indeed good, and I told her so.

19

After a delicious lunch, which no one but Susannah and I had the strength to eat, I drove into Bedford. To get there I followed State Route 96 North, keeping Buffalo Mountain on my right the entire way. It is a pretty drive, but one I hate to make. Bedford is only about ten miles from the edge of Hernia—about twelve miles from the PennDutch— but as far as I'm concerned, Bedford is light-years away.

Mama used to call it Sodom and Gomorrah, and she wasn't all wrong. Bedford has bowling alleys, bars, liquor stores, movie theaters, used-car lots, and all-night supermarkets. Susannah claims it is the last outpost of civilization, and she spends a lot of time there. I try not to go in at all, and when I do I always wear a scarf and dark glasses. I wouldn't want the devil to recognize me, after all, and follow me back to Hernia.

Today, in addition to the scarf and dark glasses I was wearing my most conservative church dress, the one I wear when, upon occasion, I attend church with Freni. This is a dark gray dress, with long sleeves, a high neckline, and a skirt that comes down well below my knees. In her more charitable moods,

Susannah calls it an "ankle chaser." Invariably I wear plain black stockings with the dress.

Since the Bedford/Hernia Yellow Pages did not list a convent, I headed straight for Saint Thomas Catholic Church on East Penn Street. They, of all people, I figured, would know where the convent was. They didn't. The woman who worked in the church office was very nice but obviously a bit confused.

"Thank God the diocese has finally sent someone to help out!" she all but shouted.

I looked around. She had to be talking to me.

"I'm Magdalena Yoder," I said quickly. "Could you tell me where the convent is?"

"Sister, the convent has been closed for years now. Surely they told you that? Well, no matter. I'm sure Father can find you a nice family to room with."

The phone rang and she excused herself to answer it. I hate it when guests eavesdrop on my calls, so I tried to be as discreet as possible by wandering over to a window and gazing intently outside. Still, I couldn't help but overhear a large part of what she said.

"Oh, the new sister will do nicely, I think. She's a big one. The kids will listen to her, I'm sure. Her name? Sister Mary Magdalena. Yeah, she's obviously of the old school. Real conservative habit. Where is she transferring from? I don't know. Let me ask."

"Excuse me," I said, before she had a chance, "I am not a nun."

"A postulant?" she asked.

"Yes, but we pronounce it 'Protestant,'" I said kindly.

Her face fell. "It's not kind to toy with us like that."

"I'm a Mennonite, dear. And the name is Magdalena, without the 'Mary' in front. I'm here because I thought you might know about the convent. The name has something to do with a broken heart."

"Oh, that." Her look of disappointment was replaced by one of sympathy. "You have a relative there?"

"No, a friend." Trust me, lies are harder to tell in a church office than at home, even if the church isn't one of your own denomination.

"Well, I certainly feel for you," the woman said sincerely. "What you're looking for is not a real convent, you know."

"It isn't?"

She shook her head vigorously. "They're some kind of New Age sect that call themselves a convent—sort of a commune for women only. But they are definitely not part of the Church."

"I see. Do you know where I can find this place? To talk to my friend, I mean. I am certainly not a candidate."

"They're somewhere up on High Street. You can't miss them, they have a wrought iron broken heart for a front gate."

"Thanks. Is there a name I should look for as well?"

"That's it. They call themselves the Convent of the Broken Heart. It's plain heresy, that's what it is. But"—she threw up her hands—"what can you do? This freedom of religion thing can be carried too far, if you ask me."

"Hear, hear," I said sincerely and thanked her for her help.

As I opened the door to leave, she called after me.

"If you ever do convert—to the Church, I mean— you'd make a damn good nun. You look the part, you know."

I walked quickly to my car. It was Wedding Day minus four, and I wasn't about to commit to a life of continued chastity, no matter how much she flattered me. Still, it was nice to know that if something ever happened to Aaron, and if I ever found myself outside the fold of my own religious heritage, there was a segment within mainline Christianity that shared not only some of my values but apparently my wardrobe as well.

I found the Convent of the Broken Heart with no trouble. It occupied an aging gray two-story frame house that was set off from the street by a narrow strip of weed-choked lawn. The broken heart on the gate was indeed obvious, once I could tear my gaze from the six-foot-high wrought iron letters that spelled the convent's name on the brown tar shingle roof. I had a much harder time trying to find the doorbell, and five minutes after I did, I concluded that it didn't work.

I knocked and got immediate results.

"Yes?" The woman who answered the door was wearing a big smile. If it hadn't been for a dirty bed sheet wrapped around her, that's all she would have been wearing—well, except for her makeup. I've seen raccoons with less eye definition.

"Is there a Sister Angelica here?" I asked politely.

She had a clear, high-pitched laugh, like the wind chimes Susannah made me hang on the back porch. "Oh, you must mean Anjelica. Sister Anjelica Huston."

"I'm sure I must. Is that perchance you?"

She tinkled a negative response. "Oh, no. I'm Sister Mary Martin. Sister Anjelica Huston is upstairs channeling."

I smiled patiently. "Well, if she wants to save a lot of time, she should head straight for Channel Six. That's where the *Green Acres* reruns are on Susannah's set."

She tinkled as if a windstorm were blowing through her porch. "Oh, not that kind of channeling, silly. Sister Anjelica Huston is the channel for Pharaoh Tutankhamen."

I had no idea what she meant, nor did I want to find out. "Can I please speak to her for a moment?"

"As herself, or as the pharaoh?"

"As herself, I suppose. Whichever one was friends with a woman named Rebecca Weaver about twenty years ago."

It was immediately obvious that one of the tinkles in Sister Mary Martin's chimes had hit a sour note. "We may be a nonprofit organization, but we do need to live, you know. Isn't there anything you wish to ask the Pharaoh? It's only twenty dollars for a three-minute session."

I fished around in my purse to see how much I was packing. "All right," I said at last, "but I'm not wearing a sheet, and I'm definitely not wearing any of that black eye makeup."

"It's kohl," she said, "and you don't have to wear any. But take off your shoes, please."

I reluctantly obeyed. I needed a new pair of black stockings desperately. If Mama saw the condition of the ones I was wearing she'd have a heart attack. Except that Mama is no longer with us, of course.

Still, I wouldn't put it past her to manage one somehow. Mama had a positive thing about keeping undergarments in good repair.

She might have had a valid point. Hannah Yutzy was hit by the mail truck while crossing Main Street in downtown Hernia. She was only grazed, and would have been all right if the paramedics hadn't insisted on giving her a thorough once-over. I'm not sure of the details, but somewhere along the line Hannah became convinced that the paramedics had discovered that her underwear was not only in need of mending but could've used a thorough bleaching as well. This realization induced hysterical paralysis, which resulted in an extended hospital stay, months of physical and psychological therapy, and an entire new wardrobe of underwear. Enough said.

Fortunately Sister Mary Martin didn't seem to notice the hole in my hose, and when I caught a glimpse of the others, I knew there was no need to worry. Hannah Yutzy could have pranced around in her dirty undies all day, and no one would have paid any attention.

The so-called nuns were seated cross-legged on the floor in a semicircle in front of one of their sisters, who was seated cross-legged on a cheap plywood-veneer coffee table. The women all turned and stared as I entered the room, and I could feel them sizing me up for a sheet-fitting.

"This"—my guide pointed to the woman on the table—"is Sister Anjelica Huston. And here"—she pointed to the rest—"we have Sister Martha Graham, Sister Debra Winger, Sister Judith Garland, Sister Margaret Mitchell, Sister Elizabeth Taylor, and Sister Cher Bono."

She didn't attempt to introduce me, but I nodded politely. "Are those your real names, dears?"

Sister Mary Martin tinkled with delight. "We of the Broken Heart leave our worldly names at the gate. In here we are free to take on whatever names we choose, provided they are grounded in the Scriptures, of course."

"Of course. In which biblical passage does the name Cher occur?" I asked pleasantly.

"Proverbs nineteen, verse eight," she said without a second's hesitation. "He who cherishes understanding prospers."

"I'm sure you do," I said kindly. "Now, I don't mean to be rude, but I have to speak to the head sister, and I haven't got all day."

Sister Mary Martin tinkled merrily. "Oh, she isn't the head sister, she's just our channeler. We have no one in authority here. It is one of our virtues." She turned to the woman on the coffee table. "Our visitor has requested to speak to Pharaoh Tutankhamen. Can it be arranged?"

"I will try," Sister Anjelica Huston said and got busy concentrating on the requisite trance.

I studied her. I assumed she was around Rebecca Weaver's age—what she would have been today— which put her near seventy. For a woman threescore and ten, she looked very well preserved. Her sheet covered a body that obviously exercised and stayed away from excessive fats. There were a few wrinkles around her eyes, but no more than I might have after a sleepless night or two. Her brown hair could well have come from a bottle, but if so, it wasn't obvious. Suddenly I began to have my doubts that Sister Anjelica Huston, aka Tutankhamen, was the same Diane Lefcourt who had been best buddies with my Pooky Bear's aunt.

"Ahmmmmmmmmmmmm!"

The woman on the coffee table was suddenly sitting ramrod straight. The women who had been sitting on the floor were now prostrate. Even Sister Mary Martin was flat on her face. For the record, I remained standing.

"His Holy Deity, Ruler of all Egypt and Upper Goshen, Lord of the Sudan and all the lands that lie beyond, Master of the Nile, Pharaoh Tutankhamen wishes to temporarily inhabit the mortal flesh of Sister Anjelica Huston!"

The speaker was the woman on the coffee table, and although she had a very deep voice, she still didn't sound like a man.

"Ahmmmmmmmmmmmmmm!" everyone hummed.

"Inhabit me, Oh Great One," Sister Anjelica Huston implored, at a much higher register.

"Ahmmmmmmmmmmmmmm!"

There was a brief period of transition, during which Sister Anjelica Huston shook and shimmied like a car with a missing spark plug, and then suddenly she was no longer there. I know that sounds crazy, but please let me explain.

Her body was, of course, still there, though even that had changed. Her skin and hair looked somehow darker, her features more pronounced, and she had every bit as many wrinkles as a California raisin. But the biggest change was in her voice. Now it did sound like a man. A man with a bass voice and a bad head cold.

"Speak, peasant!" that voice ordered.

The nuns all remained prone, barely breathing, so I assumed the command was directed at me.

"Get behind me, Satan," I said quickly. My faith frowns on seances and Ouija boards, and even if it didn't, there was definitely something spiritually unhealthy about the scene.

"What? You dare to offend Lord Tutankhamen?"

"If the shoes fits, dear," I said.

"Leave!"

"Okay, I'm out of here. But I'm not paying twenty dollars for this trash."

"Not you!" Tut roared. "Them!"

The courtiers—I'm sure none of them were vestal virgins—hopped to their feet and scampered from the room, leaving me alone with the devil himself. I backed against the wall, prepared to defend myself. Thanks to Mama and Papa, and a strict Sunday school teacher, I knew quite a few passages of the Bible by heart—and in the King James version, the one with which the Old Boy is most familiar.

"Please, relax," a woman said.

I glanced wildly around. There was no one in the room but me and a long-dead Egyptian.

"It's me."

I stared at the figure on the coffee table. The pharaoh was gone, and so was Sister Anjelica Huston. In their place was a fairly typical woman of seventy, baggy upper arms and all.

This woman uncrossed her legs stiffly and stretched them out in front of her, wiggling her toes.

"I'm baptized," I said, not about to let my guard down. "And I've brought a guardian angel or two with me, you can be sure."

My adversary chuckled. "Well, have you now? You are—?"

"Who wants to know?"

"Diane Lefcourt."

"Diane Lefcourt from Hernia? Rebecca Weaver's best friend?"

She sighed. "Yes, Becca's best friend. The one who let her down. Did you know her?"

"In a way. As a matter of fact, that's why I'm here."

She stared at me. "This has something to do with the body that was found in the pickle barrel, doesn't it? I read about it in the papers."

"That was sauerkraut. And what did you mean you let her down?"

She scooted over on the table and patted the space beside her. "Have a seat. This may take a while."

I don't mind telling you I was still somewhat shaken up by what I had witnessed and not about to share a chair with a babbling Beelzebub.

"Suit yourself, honey, but I'm quite harmless, I assure you. Now, what's your name?"

"Susannah Entwhistle." This woman, whoever she was, didn't even blink.

"Well, Susannah, Sister Mary Martin said you wanted to chat with old King Tut. I take it that's not really who you wanted to speak with?"

"No. I wanted to speak with Diane Lefcourt. Is that your real name?"

"Yeah, in a manner of speaking. I mean, I did legally change it to Sister Anjelica Huston. But I was born Diane Lefcourt."

"Well, I was born Magdalena Yoder," I confessed.

"You running from the law, honey?"

"What?"

"Never mind, I shouldn't have asked. So, what can I do for you?"

"For starters, you're not really—I mean, you don't really—"

"Go into a trance and become an antique mummy?"

"For starters."

She laughed heartily, the laugh of a seventy-year- old. "Hell, no, pardon my Egyptian. Everything you saw was an illusion."

"You mean magic? But I've been here ten minutes and you've been three different people. And you haven't even left that table!"

"Honey, I'm good at what I do. I worked in a carnival years ago. Dated the guy who ran the magic show. He talked in his sleep."

"What about the others. They know?"

She roared, then stopped suddenly, holding her finger to her lips, and nodded at the door. "Hell, no. This is the best racket there is. A permanent roof over my head and a bunch of eager disciples, all more than willing to share their earthly goods with me. Well, not me of course, but His Holy Deity Tutankhamen!"

"I could blab," I said carelessly.

She shook with mirth. "So blab. The Master of the Nile has already warned them about false prophets. Now, what is it you want? Tell me, before the Ruler of Upper Goshen turns you into a frog."

I decided to let the brokenhearted temple maidens with the fanciful names fend for themselves. At least temporarily.

"Sarah Weaver's funeral is tomorrow afternoon. At Beechy Grove Mennonite Church. You're welcome to attend, if you still own a dress. Her entire family will be there, even her dad, who I managed to locate in Florida."

"Jonas?"

"Yes. Anyway, it's become very obvious to me that whoever killed Sarah killed Rebecca too, and—"

"Nobody killed Rebecca," she said.

"What?" I stared at her. She was still in her Diane persona and looked quite serious.

"I said, nobody killed my friend Becca."

"That's nonsense, dear," I said gently. "No one has seen her for twenty years, and her own daughter—"

"No one killed her," Diane growled in a voice not unlike Tutankhamen's. "I know, because I've seen her. In fact, I saw her just last week."

I sat down on the coffee table. If she was indeed the devil, or if the table buckled and crashed to the floor, so be it. My legs weren't designed for megashocks.

"What do you mean you saw her last week?" I finally gasped.

She had the nerve to pat me in a motherly way. "Get a grip on it, honey. I saw her over in Harrisburg. I go to see her every month. She's in a mental hospital."

I let that soak in. Then I thought about asking her if the Harrisburg hospital had any vacancies, but I was afraid I might be misunderstood. It was me I wanted to admit, not her.

"What's the name of the hospital?"

She shook her head. "That's privileged information. I've already told you far too much. I just wanted you to know that Becca isn't dead."

"But, but—does Jonas know this?"

"Hell, no! And you're not going to tell him, are you? Because if you do, I'll deny it. And don't try calling the hospitals either, because they won't find her. And anyway, maybe she isn't in Harrisburg. Maybe I made that part up."

It sounded almost like a challenge, and I didn't know what to think. Then I remembered Sarah's diary.

"Well, according to Sarah's diary, her mother is dead. She saw it happen, you know. It's all down on paper."

Diane Lefcourt stared at me, becoming more and more like Tutankhamen with every passing second. "Sarah saw something. But it wasn't her mother being killed. So, whose word are you going to take for it, mine or little Sarah's?"

"Little Sarah's," I said, but I wasn't so sure.

I started to leave, but she grabbed my arm with a hand that was amazingly strong. "How did you find me anyway?"

I pried her fingers loose. They may as well have belonged to a resuscitated mummy. They were as cold as ice.

"I called information and took a chance on the only Lefcourt in Johnstown. It was your son. Does he know what you do for a living?"

She laughed, suddenly not caring if the others heard or not. "Someone once said there is a sucker born every minute. You, honey, are the biggest lollipop I know."

I stormed out of there without paying my twenty bucks.

20

Magdalena Yoder's Wedding Feast, from Soup to Nuts

Auntie Magdalena's Potato Dumplings

3 cups mashed potatoes (cooled)
2 eggs
1 cup flour
1 teaspoon salt
½ teaspoon onion powder
2 quarts chicken or vegetable broth (water may be used in
place of part or all). If only water is used, compensate by
adding a teaspoon of salt, melted butter

Thoroughly mix eggs, flour, salt, and onion powder into cool mashed potatoes. Let mixture sit for a few minutes while liquid is brought to a rolling boil. Shape potato mixture into balls approximately 1½ inches in diameter. Cook on high heat until dumplings begin to rise to the top of the pot, then simmer until cooked through center. Drain and drizzle with melted butter to prevent dumplings from sticking to each other.

Note: Try cooking one dumpling first to see if it holds together. If it comes apart, add more flour.

Serves 4.

21

The last thing I needed when I got back to the PennDutch was to find Melvin Stoltzfus sitting in his squad car in my driveway. Zelda was sitting there with him, looking like something the cat had dragged in, played with for a few days, and then discarded. The woman was wearing a zebra-striped bathrobe, for Pete's sake. If Zelda was that sick she should have stayed home in bed with an old sock tied around her neck. There are few things that a little Vicks rubbed into the throat won't cure.

"Well, well, well," Melvin said gleefully, as he clambered out of his car. Poor Zelda stayed behind, undoubtedly too sick to care.

"I am in no mood for niceties, Melvin, so spit it out."

"You're skating on thin ice as it is, Yoder. I advise you not to push your luck."

"Melvin, dear, it's the middle of June. The pond has long since melted."

"Exactly, Yoder. This little visit is way overdue."

I walked past him. "I already have guests," I called over my shoulder. "You're going to have to take a number."

He had the nerve to laugh. He sounded like a choir of cacophonous katydids.

"Hold it right there, Yoder. I have a search warrant for these premises."

I whirled around. "You what?"

If you haven't seen a praying mantis smile, you haven't missed much. "Here." He waved a piece of paper. "A properly executed warrant to search the PennDutch and outlying buildings. It's all legal."

"To search for what? I sent the Peruvian nanny packing last week, and my Colombian drug shipment isn't due in until Thursday."

"Very funny, Yoder. I'm here to look for the victim's diary. I also have a warrant to search your person."

"My what?"

"Your person. That means you—your body."

"Touch me and die, Melvin." I know, those aren't the words that should spring from the lips of a twelfth-generation pacifist, but since Melvin has the power to turn Mother Teresa into an ax murderess, I couldn't help myself.

He spread his mandibles into a wide, mocking grin. "Well, I don't have to touch you, now, do I? That's why I brought Zelda with me. Zelda!"

Melvin had to call four times before she heard him. Although Zelda was a zonked zombie, nonetheless she zigzagged zealously toward us on her zebra-striped zoris.

"What are you searching for?" I demanded of Melvin.

"As if you don't know," he sneered.

"No, I don't!" I screamed in frustration. "I don't carry diaries around on my person."

"Well, play dumb, then, Yoder. It's your call."

By then Zelda had zeroed in on us and was swaying precariously. She was clearly in no shape to pat anything, except maybe a pillow. It would be a piece of cake to push her over and then make a mad dash for my car. Thanks to the inn, and my ebullient personality, I had friends in every state but one.

"Don't even think about it, Yoder," Melvin snarled. "I'll do it myself. The law says I can if I have a female officer in attendance."

"Ahhhhhhhhhhhhhhhhhhhhhhhhhh!"

As he reached for me I let out a scream that woke the dead in nine counties and dried up dairy herds two states away. Susannah told me later that she was very proud of me. A world-class scream, she said. I could easily qualify for the International Sisters in Screams Competition to be held in Acapulco sometime the following spring.

Aaron heard me scream as well. He was on his way over for supper, along with his father, and he ditched Pops to come to my rescue. He said he immediately knew it was me. No one else in Bedford County had lungs with that capacity or a range that could simultaneously shatter glass and get the bullfrogs croaking.

My Pooky Bear, my hero, arrived just as I let out a second scream, this time with words.

"Get your grubby hands off me, Melvin Stoltzfus!"

"You heard her," Aaron roared.

Actually, if truth be told, Aaron spoke very calmly. Far too calmly for a man whose sugar dumpling has almost been violated by a deviant detective.

Still, Melvin seemed stymied. He scratched his head longer than a flea-prone dog in a henhouse.

"Well," he said at last, "then I'm just going to have to take you in to the station and search you there."

"On what grounds?" Aaron asked sensibly.

"Obstruction of justice," Melvin said and reached to snap a pair of cuffs on me.

Make no mistake about it, I am claustrophobic. Not about tight spaces necessarily, but about being physically restrained. I cannot abide constrictive apparel of any sort. For this reason, I won't even wear a watch unless I absolutely have to. So you see, when I felt that cold, confining metal circle my wrist, it was a reflex pure and simple that caused me to fling my arm outward. And it was pure bad luck that made my fist connect with Melvin's miserable mug.

Contrary to Susannah's claims, I do not possess big muscles. I do not use steroids, nor have I ever used them. In gym class I could never get past two pushups, and I couldn't do a chin-up if my life depended on it. But somehow I managed to lay Melvin out like a salami at an Italian picnic.

I didn't lay a hand on Zelda, though. If it wasn't against my religion, I'd swear to that on a stack of Farmer's Almanacs. The fact that she hit the driveway just seconds after Melvin had to be due to her bad cold. I mean, I didn't even graze her. As for the charge that I stuck out my foot and tripped her—well, I'd have to say that is complete nonsense. I stuck out my foot because impacting Melvin's mandibles caused me to lose my balance. And that is the truth. A healthy woman would not have gone down so easily.

I had never been inside a jail before, and in a way it was more interesting than it was scary. Like I said, I can handle relatively small spaces—it's being shackled that makes me flip.

Hernia has separate cells for the sexes, and apparently the women's cell doesn't get much use. There were only four names scratched into the walls, not including Susannah's, and the mattress and pillow, while lumpy, were quite clean. I wish I could say the same about the toilet, although in all fairness its brown color was undoubtedly because of the hard water. After all, the sink was brown as well. Of course it was a peculiar toilet, in that it had actually been designed not to have a seat. Only a man could think that one up, I assure you.

There were four bunks, and I chose a top one on the off chance I would be getting company. I was just settling down to collect my wits when I heard the hall door open and two sets of footsteps approach. I closed my eyes and prayed for strength.

"Brought you some company," a female voice said. It was Andrea, Zelda's replacement, on loan from Bedford.

"Just remember I was here first, dearie," I said in my gruffest voice. "You don't mess with me, I don't mess with you."

"Ach! Magdalena Yoder, how you talk!"

"Freni!" I opened my eyes and sat up.

"Who else? Were you expecting the sewing circle from church?"

"Freni, you didn't hit Melvin too, did you?"

"Ach! Of course not! I'm here to visit. Magdalena, if your mother could1—"

"Please," I begged. "For once leave Mama out of it. Are you here to bail me out?"

She shook her head. She was wearing her black traveling bonnet, which looked rather out of place behind the bars.

"Aaron can't post bail until tomorrow morning, after the hearing. You're going to have to spend the night in here, I'm afraid."

"But it wasn't my fault!" I wailed. "You know Melvin Stoltzfus. Doesn't that say it all?"

Freni nodded sympathetically. "Yah, but assaulting a police officer—make that two police officers—is serious business, Magdalena. Melvin is talking about having you tell time."

"You must mean 'do' time," I corrected her gently. "Freni, you know I can't stay in here. I've got a murder to solve, not to mention a wedding—my wedding—on Saturday." I glanced over at Andrea, who was discreetly looking away. "You and Aaron have to get me out, Freni," I whispered.

Freni looked at me fondly with her faded blue eyes. That was as close as she could come to saying "I love you."

"How, Magdalena?"

"I don't know. Bring me a cake with a file baked inside. Sneak a gun in under your bonnet. Just get me out, and soon!"

Freni nodded pensively. "There may be a way," she said. "There just may be a way."

But she wouldn't tell me more.

Susannah was my next visitor. She seemed right at home.

"I usually take that bunk over there," she said brightly. "The mattress is better."

"Where?"

She hauled Shnookums out of her cleavage and set him on the floor. The pathetic pooch slipped right through the bars and headed straight for the bottom bunk on the other side of the room. Somehow it managed to hop up on the bed, and, in an attack of nervous exuberance, piddled pitifully on the pillow.

"They allow you to bring him in here?" I asked calmly. Andrea was safely engrossed in the latest issue of Cosmopolitan (which, I learned later, Susannah had provided as a diversion).

"Yeah, but I've never been hauled in for assault and battery, Mags. Disturbing the peace is as far as I've gotten—if you don't count DWI—and that was only twice. Besides, Melvin and me used to be friends, remember?"

"I'd rather not, dear, but now that you've brought up the subject, I don't suppose you'd be willing to impose on your bond to see that I make mine. I am supposed to be married on Saturday, you know."

Susannah rolled her eyes in sympathy. "Yeah. Bummer. But Melvin hates my guts now, Mags, since I dumped him. Says I broke his heart down to the bone, which sounds kind of silly to me. Hearts don't have bones, do they, Mags?"

"Melvin's does," I said. "Are you sure there's nothing you can do or say?"

She shook her head vigorously, no doubt admiring the way her hair looked in the reflection of the bars. "He says only Zelda can do it now for him, Mags, and you knocked her out cold."

"I did not!"

I froze while Andrea glanced around the room and then buried her head back in other women's cleavage.

"She was sick, Susannah. Shnookums could have toppled her over."

"Well, you're still my hero, you know."

"What?" I hadn't been so shocked since that time I was sent home from school early because of an approaching snowstorm and found Mama and Papa in a flagrante delicto. Well, their version of it, anyway. Papa was down to his long johns and Mama was in her flannel nightie. But it was broad daylight outside!

"Come on, Mags, don't make me say it twice."

"Please."

"Okay, but then this is the last time. You're my hero, all right? I mean, I've always looked up to you—because you're my big sister—but now I really respect you."

"Because I punched Melvin out?"

"And Zelda."

I held my tongue that time. If Susannah wanted to believe that I had intentionally clobbered two cops, who was I to rain on her parade?

"So, can I get you anything?" my sweet little sister asked.

"My Bible," I said seriously.

She nodded just as seriously. "Shall I carve out a little space and hide a knife in it?"

I patted her arm affectionately through the bars. "Thanks, but no thanks. You excited about your first day at work tomorrow?"

She shrugged, but I could tell by the sudden gleam in her eyes that she was immensely excited. Would wonders never cease! My slothful, slatternly sister was about to embark on an endeavor for which she could expect to receive legal remuneration. Our parents would be so proud.

"You're not planning to smuggle Shnookums in with you?" I asked casually.

"Of course!"

"But Susannah, what if that pint-size canine falls into a can of paint? He could drown."

She looked taken aback. "Why, I hadn't thought of that, Mags. I suppose there is some risk, after all."

"You're damn tootin', dear," I said affectionately. I was growing prouder by the moment.

"So, in that case, I think you should keep him."

Without another word, my sister turned in a swirl of shimmering silk and slipped out of the holding area. Andrea, who had forgotten to lock the door, darted after her in a panic. Perhaps she thought I had slipped Susannah a dangerous weapon.

In the meantime Shnookums, who had all the pet appeal of a rabid rat, began to howl piteously. I really couldn't blame the mangy mutt. Susannah had hand-reared him on a doll's bottle after his mother had refused to nurse him (I couldn't blame her either!). Except for one time last year when a vicious man in Ohio came between them for several days, the two had been inseparable.

Anyway, much to my credit, I petted the pooch.

"It's okay, my sweetsie-beastie, itsy-bitsy little Shnookums," I cooed in my most Susannah-like voice.

The mangy mutt rewarded me by mashing his minuscule yet menacing molars down on my right index finger.

That did it. It had been too horrible and long of a day to be harassed by a hair ball.

"Get this straight, buster," I shouted. "You keep that yap of yours shut or I'll turn you into a dust mop. You got that?"

Shnookums blinked, but said nothing.

"I read you loud and clear," my Pooky Bear said.

22

"Hi Aaron!" I glanced around for someplace to hide, but the only hole available to crawl into was the lidless brown toilet.

"You're quite a woman, you know?" If I had been brave enough to look, I would have seen that my Pooky Bear's eyes were gleaming with admiration.

"I only punched Melvin. Zelda tripped—well, sort of."

"And they say chivalry is dead! Imagine that, my very own hellcat to do battle for me. You'll make one hell of a protective mother, Magdalena. Our kids will be the safest ones on the lane."

"Our kids," I wailed, "are going to be born in jail!"

Aaron laughed. "Then with these bars they'll even have extra protection."

I failed to see the humor in his comments and told him so. He pretended to be chastised but wouldn't stop grinning.

"Look, you'll be out of here first thing in the morning. Judge Wagler is the magistrate and—"

"Jacob Wagler?"

"You know him?"

"Unfortunately, quite well."

"Oh, Mags," my Pooky Bear sighed, "you didn't hit him too, did you?"

"Worse than that. I made him eat dirt."

"Figuratively, of course, but I'm sure—"

"No, literally. We were three years old at the time. Actually, he was already four. Anyway, we were playing in a sandbox—my sandbox—and he grabbed my shovel and wouldn't give it back. So I pushed him down, sat on top of him, and fed him dirt."

"You made him eat dirt?" Aaron's voice echoed down the hall, and Andrea momentarily surfaced from a sea of anorexic women with breast implants.

"Aaron, what else was I supposed to do?" I wailed. "There were only two shovels, and he already had the other!"

I stole a quick glance at my fiancé's face, and that was when I noticed that his eyes were shining. They were just brimming over with love.

"I've waited a whole lifetime to find a woman like you, Mags," he said. "I sure as hell am not going to let a repugnant runt like Melvin Stoltzfus delay our happiness by even one day."

"You go, boy," I said, borrowing one of Susannah's favorite phrases.

"I'll move heaven and earth if that's what it takes," my hero declared stoutly. "I'll climb the highest mountain, I'll—"

"Will you keep a mangy mutt overnight?" I scooped Shnookums off his bunk and thrust him through the bars.

It was the true test of my Pooky Bear's love that he gingerly accepted the cowering cur and stuffed him into the vest pocket of his shirt.

"Till tomorrow, my love," he said.

Let me make it perfectly clear here that it was Aaron who spoke, not Shnookums. That mangy, malodorous mutt just yelped piteously while Andrea, without looking up from her magazine, unlocked the hall door and let them out.

Think me strange, but I actually enjoyed my night in jail. Once I got it through my head that I was really stuck there, alone, it didn't take me long to discover all the advantages solitary confinement has to offer.

For one thing, I had four beds to choose from, and I could rotate among them all night long if I so desired. Of course, at the PennDutch I have more than four beds, but the majority of them are perennially occupied by the rich and famous (present occupants excluded) who fill my coffers, and I'm not about to kick them out of bed when I want a change of mattress.

The real blessing, however, was the sudden and complete lack of responsibility I felt. If Susannah decided to drink and flirt her way up to Poughkeepsie, there was nothing I could do about it. Just as long as she didn't end up sharing my cell that night, my dear little sister was none of my concern.

And, of course, neither were my guests. Let Freni quit, let Auntie Leah bellow in the kitchen, let Auntie Vonnie gripe. Auntie Lizzie could paint herself up as the whore of Babylon for all I cared, and if Auntie Magdalena whimpered herself into a frenzy, well, that was somebody else's problem, wasn't it? As for the uncles, who cared if they slept all night in the parlor—although it would be nice if Uncle Elias got on the ball and checked out the Millers' barn.

It was even pleasant, in a weird sort of way, to be cut off from my Pooky Bear. I mean, he had said such sweet things during his visit, and since my cell didn't have a phone, there was no chance he would make a late-night call. My tongue is the least reliable of my appendages, and has been known to double-cross me more than once. Much better to end the evening with my Pooky Bear's eyes brimming with admiration than to struggle through a phone call during which I—the Lord only knows for what reason— might suddenly start talking about barium enemas and throbbing varicose veins. Not that such abrupt turns in conversation have necessarily happened, mind you, but it was a big relief to be freed from the risk.

I slept like a baby, which is to say I woke up every couple of hours. Finally, I forced myself to squat over the brown toilet, after which sleep stayed with me. In fact, I was enjoying the deepest sleep I'd had in years when Melvin Stoltzfus began banging on the door to my cell with a cluster of keys.

"Go away," I moaned.

"Yoder, get up!"

I sat up, rubbing my eyes. "There'd better be a breakfast tray in your other hand, dear. This place has done wonders for my appetite."

He unlocked the door, opened it, and stepped back. "Out."

"Oh? It's the shower first? Listen, Melvin, I washed my hair yesterday, and I'm quite content to wait and take a good soak when I get home."

"Yoder, out!"

There was something odd about his voice, something that compelled me to look at him closely. I recoiled at the sight. Melvin Stoltzfus had a black eye. I mean a real shiner, the kind they tell you to put steak on, which is a real waste, because the steak would make you and your eye feel a whole lot better faster if you charbroiled it and ate it. Only in Melvin's case, given the size of his ocular orbs, it was doubtful he could afford that much meat.

"Ooooh. Did I do that?" I asked gently.

Much to my surprise he laughed loudly. "Don't be so full of yourself, Yoder. You hit me in the chest and I lost my balance. This I got later. Much later."

"Aaron? If you've arrested Aaron—"

"I didn't arrest your precious Aaron. Now come on, Yoder. You have some papers to sign."

"I'm not signing anything until after my day in court. Which reminds me, Jacob Wagler is going to have to disqualify himself on account I once made him eat dirt."

"There isn't going to be any court hearing, Yoder. And as for Judge Wagler, he said he'd rather eat dirt again than touch you with a ten-foot pole."

"What? You can't just ship me off to the state pen without a trial! It's unconstitutional, Melvin! Why, if your mother—" At the mention of his mother, Melvin seemed to wilt.

"Please, Yoder. Just come."

"Why, Melvin Stoltzfus, what on earth is going on? Did your mother—? I mean, did Freni—?"

He nodded dejectedly, and I almost felt sorry for him. Only one woman in the world has more control over her children than my mother (God rest her soul, and Susannah excepted), and that's Elvina Stoltzfus. Poor Melvin was born with a steel umbilical cord, and nothing he will ever do, including die, will sever it.

While I am experiencing this rare moment of compassion for my nemesis, I will go ahead and say that it is to Melvin's credit that he is who he is. What I mean is, if Elvina Stoltzfus had had her way, Melvin would still be incapable of feeding himself, much less walking or talking. Those of us who observed Melvin's relative maturation were astounded when he began to date (his brother Perry is reportedly still very fond of a sheep named Delilah). So, for all the grief that Melvin gives me, it could be worse, I suppose. After all, Elvina Stoltzfus would follow her precious son everywhere, I'm sure, if it were not for the ten-pound goiter attached to her neck, which she firmly refuses to have removed. Then again, that's her business, isn't it?

I successfully resisted my temptation to pat him compassionately. "Was it your mother who gave you the shiner, dear?"

"But it was really your fault, Magdalena."

"How so?"

"You sicced Freni Hostetler on me."

"I did no such thing, dear. I merely agreed that she should speak to your mother."

He tried glaring, but it was obviously painful. "You knew that Freni and Mama are as close as two peas in a pod."

"Black-eyed peas?"

"Very funny, Yoder. When Freni Hostetler got done bending Mama's ear, Mama began twisting mine. And I mean that literally. 'You let that poor little Magdalena go,' she said. 'You drop those charges at once. Don't you know she's getting married Saturday?'

" 'Like I care?' I said. That's when Mama threw her wooden darning egg at me."

"Looks like child abuse to me," I said sympathetically.

"She didn't mean to hit me, you know! Mama would never mean to hurt her little Mellykins."

I decided that Melvin was wounded enough. There was no need to bait him further. If I were half the woman my Aaron thought I was, I would have gathered Melvin Stoltzfus in my arms and rocked him like the baby Aaron so badly wanted. But I am only human, and although he may never realize it, my gift to him that day was that I shut my mouth when I did and kept it shut for as long as I did.

Without a peep I obediently signed a paper stating that I understood charges had been dropped and another one saying that I was leaving with the same worldly goods with which I had arrived.

"Sam Yoder has a special going on sirloin," I said kindly, as I was taking my leave.

Melvin's good eye rotated slowly in my direction. "Freni Hostetler will not always be around to protect you, Yoder. Someday—just you wait. Someday!"

"Well, ta-ta," I said and started to skip to the door. And then I remembered something vitally important.

"About Jonas's diary—"

"The one you stole?"

I let that pass. "Did you—ah—did you get a chance to search the inn?"

"You can bet your farm I did, Yoder, and with a fine-tooth comb." He sounded much stronger now, much more in control of himself now that he had done his mother's bidding.

"Well, did you find it?"

"That's for me to know and you to find out."

I sighed patiently. "Melvin, dear, if indeed I had taken it—which, I assure you, I didn't—I would find out the second I got home, wouldn't I? So, if I were the thief, I wouldn't ask, would I? And anyway, if I were the thief—which I'm not—you would have a good reason to arrest me, even aside from our little altercation of last night. Right?"

He considered that for a moment. "You really should stay out of police business, Yoder. We'd all be much better off if you left things up to us professionals."

I caught myself before I'd completed a full eye roll. "I'm sure you have a point, dear. However, I have a lot of stake in this particular case. You didn't perhaps, search Jonas Weaver's things, did you?"

Melvin curtailed his laugh when it began to some-how hurt his eye. "Why would Jonas Weaver steal his own daughter's diary? He already had it, didn't he?"

"He had it, all right. I know that, because I read it. But I'm the only one who read it. Maybe there's something in there he suddenly decided he doesn't want anyone to know. Maybe he decided not to cooperate after all. Then it would be just his word against mine."

"So?"

"So, whose word would you believe? Jonas Weaver's or mine?"

I had given Melvin a chance to be gracious, but it was obviously too much for him. "I'd believe Mr. Weaver," he said without a second's hesitation. "Anyway, you're not making a lick of sense, Yoder. It was Jonas Weaver's wife and daughter who were murdered. Why would he refuse to cooperate?"

"Maybe he did it!" I screamed. Trust me, as screams go, this one was fairly restrained, if not downright cultured. Aaron told me later that he did not hear it back at the inn.

Melvin laughed again until his eye made him quit, and then he told me to call Aaron and ask him to come pick me up. After that, despite the depth of emotion we had just shared, Melvin rudely showed me the door. He wisely avoided putting his hands on me this time, and I wisely kept mine dug deep into the pockets of my dress.

"Bye-bye, Yoder," he said, as if I were a child.

"Don't forget that the funeral is this afternoon at three, dear," I graciously reminded him.

For a split second I had a glimpse of the vulnerable Melvin, the one who had known and cared about Sarah Weaver. Then, like that little metal door at the ATM machine, a shield came down and blocked off his emotions. His good emotions, I mean.

"I can charge you with loitering," he said, "so I suggest you wait outside for your boyfriend."

I smiled. "And while I'm waiting, I hope you have fun looking for the limerick I carved into the wall. It's all about you and Susannah."

"You didn't!"

I hadn't, But I found out later that Susannah had, and in a place I would never have thought to look. But that's another story.

23

"What?"

"Get in," Unde Elias said. "Aaron couldn't make it."

"But I just spoke to him. Minutes ago. He said he'd be here in a flash."

"Well, something came up. An emergency. So I volunteered." He patted the passenger seat. "Are you just going to stand there, or what?"

I climbed in. "What kind of emergency? It isn't Freni, is it? That dear old woman came out to see me last night—"

"It isn't Freni. Last I saw of her she was giving Leah what for. Vonnie too. No, this didn't seem to be of the medical type. There was a phone call from Reverend Schrock, and then young Aaron just said he had to go. Said he might be gone a long time and not to hold lunch. He took big Aaron with him."

"Merciful heavens, it's the wedding, then! If that whippersnapper decided to cancel the wedding and take off fishing, I'll see to it that he's disrobed—defrocked—you know what I mean. Just because I'm a jailbird doesn't mean I can't marry Aaron. Does it?" I wailed.

Uncle Elias chuckled. "I don't think you qualify as a jail-bird, Magdalena, and anyway, I'm pretty sure this doesn't have to do with the wedding. It's about the funeral. Something about the grave."

I leaned back and gasped for air. "Well, in that case let's head straight for the church. The gravesite is out back in the Weaver family plot."

Just then Melvin came racing up behind us in Hernia's only police car, his lights flashing, and his siren whining. Uncle Elias obligingly started to pull over, but Melvin went zipping around us and sped off down the road. He didn't appear to be interested in us in the least. I slid down low in my seat anyway.

"Crime must be rampant in Hernia lately," Uncle Elias joked. "And speaking of which, I did a little breaking and enter-ing myself last night and found something rather interesting."

I had to push my heart back into my chest a few times before I could talk. "You went over and checked out Pops's barn liked I suggested?"

"Bingo."

"You found Rebecca?"

He chuckled again. "I'm not superman. I don't have X-ray vision, and I couldn't very well dig in the dark. We have to wait until the time is right—until nobody's there and we can see what we're doing. Like now, don't you think?"

"Now?"

"It may be our only chance if you want to get this settled by Saturday. Think about it—it's perfect. Aaron and his father will be gone for quite a while, and anyway you can stand guard and warn me if they come back before I'm done."

"What will I tell them?" I wailed.

"That's what you get to think up while you're standing guard."

"But what about Freni and the others? Won't they think it's odd if you don't bring me right home?"

He shook his head. "No, that's the beauty of it. Aaron, his dad, and I were alone in the lobby when you called. Reverend Schrock called the second you hung up. Nobody else knows a thing."

"Well, we'll need tools, won't we? And they're back at the PennDutch, so we'll have to stop there first. Someone's bound to see us."

He jabbed a thumb over his shoulder. "Got the tools. Grabbed them from your tool shed on my way out. You've got quite a setup."

"They were my father's," I said glumly.

There was nothing I could do but acquiesce. After all, searching the barn had been my idea. If standing guard on my own fiancé's farm while an elderly uncle dug around for a skeleton was going to expedite closure of the grim situation, then so be it. First jailbird, and then gang lookout—well, somebody had to do it.

We fought our way through a sea of cats and into the barn. Fortunately Cyrus, the cat that had gotten amorous on my lap, had found herself a tom she liked and was busy doing unspeakable things, but at least not on me. The barn looked the same to me as it had the last time, benign and empty, and for a fleeting and shameful second, I began to doubt Uncle Elias's intentions.

"I'm spoken for, you know," I said as he led me to a far corner.

He stared at me blankly for a moment and then burst into loud guffaws. "You? You and me? Get serious!"

"Well, I never!"

"Exactly. I have no interest in a colt that hasn't been broken in. Give me a mare that can take it to the finish every time."

"You better be meaning Auntie Magdalena," I said.

"You're damn right I do. That woman is all the woman I will ever need, and then some. Yesiree, she's a real thoroughbred. First around the track half the time, and then, like as not, takes an extra lap or two."

His fidelity pleased me, but his frankness shocked me. If he meant what I thought he meant, then drab, whimpering Auntie Magdalena was just like Cyrus the cat. I was profoundly embarrassed and silently resolved to think of a way to avoid direct eye contact with either of the Fikes ever again. Yet in a strange way—and this is strictly confidential—I was happy that my namesake could not only make it around the track but come in first. I'd been worrying that I might not even have what it takes to get out of the starting gate and that the pope, or someone like him, would have to annul my marriage. Susannah would never let me live that down.

"Well, show me what you've got," I said briskly, and then realizing my double entendre, did a thorough turn.

Uncle Elias didn't even seem to notice. He dropped the tools on the floor with a loud thunk.

"Look over there," he said, pointing to the comer.

I looked. "Yes?"

"Those floorboards. They're different from the others, see? They're a different kind of wood, and they're narrower."

"So?"

"I think maybe it's a trapdoor." He got down on his hands and knees and began blowing the dust away from the area where the two wood types adjoined. "Yep, here's where the hinges are. You can barely see them because they're on the other side. Pretty clever. Hand me the crowbar, will you?"

I picked up the crowbar he had just thrown down. I am not mechanically minded, but since I was the oldest daughter, and for a long time the only child, Papa had made sure I had a working familiarity with your basic garden-variety tools.

Uncle Elias slid the beveled prongs of the crowbar along the line of his so-called trapdoor, gently testing it now and then for give. It didn't budge.

"There must be a hidden catch somewhere that I'm missing. Here, you try it."

"Shouldn't I be standing guard?" I asked nervously.

Even as I was still speaking I heard a faint click and the door—for, indeed, that's what it was— opened a crack. I pried it higher, got both sets of fingers in there, and hoisted it aloft. It was heavy, and I got a snootful of dust, but we had hit pay dirt. So to speak.

"Well, I'll be damned," Uncle Elias said, leaning over the edge. "It's a little cellar of some kind."

It certainly was, if you were a dwarf. It was impossible to even kneel in the little space, much less stand. And although there was a pair of wooden steps going down, they led to nothing.

"Apparently when Snow White moved out, she took everything with her," I said bitterly. "What on earth do we do now?"

Uncle Elias sat down on the edge of the hole and dangled his feet. Even as short as he was, they almost touched the bottom.

"Well, now, let me think."

While he thought, I trotted over to the bam door and peered out. Aaron's truck wasn't back. I had half expected to see it.

"Silly me," I chided myself. "If he was back he would have seen my car, and not finding me in it, or around the yard, he just might have tried the barn. There he would have found me with Uncle Elias and a bunch of tools, tearing up the floor. What was I thinking?"

"You say something?" Uncle Elias called.

Instead of answering right away, I dashed out and peered around the comer of the barn. The Miller drive was empty and there were no cars at all on Hertzler Lane. I sprinted back to the scene of the crime.

"We have to go," I cried. "If my Pooky Bear finds me here like this, how will I ever explain it? Please, we have to go!"

Uncle Elias ignored my passionate pleas for sanity. He got up and tested the first step. It held up, but it wouldn't have made much difference if it hadn't. How bad can you hurt yourself by falling two feet?

"Hand me the shovel," he ordered. "The one with the pointed mouth."

I passed him the tool. "You think there's a body in there? Why would someone bury a body and then go to all the trouble of building a trapdoor? Wouldn't it make more sense to seal up the floor permanently?"

He began scraping the top layer of dirt gently aside. "It would make perfect sense if you planned to bury more than one body, and at different times."

"You don't mean it?" I plopped down at the edge of the hole. My toes would have touched the bottom, but I was careful not to let them.

"Yep," Uncle Elias said. "I read about something just like this in the St. Louis papers. Only it involved an attic. The killer was a woman and all her victims were men. Postmen. She killed off four or five of them, one by one, over a period of years, and somehow managed to drag them up a folding stairway and stash them in the attic."

"She must have been a big woman," I said.

"My Magdalena could do it, that's for damn sure. Why once in the throes of passion—"

"I don't want to hear it!" I clamped my hands tightly over my ears.

Uncle Elias had to dig in silence, which was just as well. I had decided to listen, rather than look, for Aaron's truck. If and when I heard it, we would throw the rest of the tools in the pit and close the trapdoor. If questioned about my whereabouts or activities. I would tell my Pooky Bear that I had decided to give him a motorcycle for his wedding present and had come over to check out his barn as a place to store it until after the ceremony. After all, I figured, he spent more time at the inn than he did at home, and weren't gifts displayed right under one's nose always the last ones discovered? It was a lame excuse, but it was all I could manage on an empty stomach. Melvin had refused to invest any of the county's money in a prisoner who was being released so early in the morning. As for Uncle Elias's excuse for being there, that was his problem.

"Well, I'll be damned," Uncle Elias said loudly.

I took my hands off my ears. "Now what? You find Dopey?"

"Maybe. Just maybe I have!"

I leaned forward. Uncle Elias had uncovered a piece of burlap and was very gently scraping dirt from it with the point of the shovel. Shivers ran up my spine.

"You don't think that's Rebecca, do you?"

Uncle Elias was concentrating too intently to answer. But I already knew the answer, so it didn't matter. Of course it was Rebecca down there. At least her killer had considerately wrapped her in a burlap shroud and buried her in out of the rain. No doubt he would have buried Sarah there too, but something unexpected must have come up and he had been forced to stash her hastily in the barrel of kraut.

But how could the killer get away with installing a trap-door in Pops's barn unless—the killer was Pops! It had to be. He was the only logical choice. He might even have built the trapdoor and secret compartment well in advance of that anniversary week. Sure, the space beneath the floor was shallow, but it was a big door, at least six feet square. Depending on whether or not he intended to stack his victims beneath the soil, Pops Miller could have done away with any number of his guests that fateful summer, the Beeftrust included.

But his own sisters? Well, that's what Rebecca was to him. And Sarah was his niece. Apparently blood meant nothing to the man. And he had the nerve to all but invite himself to come and live with me. I would have to check my barn for trapdoors now that he'd been spending so much time over there with Aaron.

It was a horrible revelation. Too gruesome to contemplate for more than a few seconds, but it made perfect sense now. No wonder Pops was so upset about having to sell his farm. He was afraid that his earthen death pit would be discovered. Or was he? Maybe it was all an act. Maybe he was looking forward to its discovery. After all, he had been the one to send over the barrel of sauerkraut for my wedding. Maybe he was away that morning in hopes that it would be discovered. Maybe he had doubled back and was gleefully watching us at that very moment. Undoubtedly we were intended to be his next victims. Pops the psychopath!

Of course, that was silly since Pops was with his son, Aaron, and it had been Aaron who had gotten the phone call from Rev. Schrock demanding his presence. That would only work if—

"Oh, no!" I wailed. "Not my Pooky Bear!"

"Hot damn, would you look at that!"

I shook myself free from my morbid reverie, but I refused to look. I am not a rubbemecker. If there is nothing I can do to help at the scene of an accident, I will drive right past it without looking. Garnering stimulation from other folks' misery is just plain wrong. I had absolutely no desire to look at the remains of Rebecca Weaver. Anyway, seeing her daughter, Sarah, in a sauerkraut barrel was quite enough. I was sure the sight of Rebecca couldn't hold a candle to that.

"Uh-oh! I see you've found it," I heard someone say. Someone other than Uncle Elias, that is.

I scrabbled around, grabbing at the tools, but it was too late. Both of the Miller men were framed against the barn door. They were in silhouette, so I couldn't see their expressions, but no doubt their faces were twisted in rage.

"I—I didn't see anything!" I stammered. "Nothing, I tell you. And it was Uncle Elias's idea."

"Elias, you knew all along?" Pops asked rather calmly.

"Hell, no," Uncle Elias said, and he laughed. Laughed!

I turned to give him a righteous glare, and that's when I saw the bottles. Dozens of bottles.

"Where's the body?" I gasped.

"Body?"

My Aaron laughed and ran a hand through his thick black hair. "My Magdalena has quite an imagination, doesn't she?"

"Boy, I'll say," Uncle Elias agreed far too heartily.

"Well, now," Pops said, "now that you've found my stash, Elias, what do you plan to do?"

"Damn you, Aaron," Uncle Elias said, "I knew you were holding out on me all these years, but this is something else."

Pops looked him straight in the eye. "You aren't going to tell, are you?"

"You up to sharing?" Uncle Elias asked.

Pops considered that for a moment and nodded.

I jumped up and grabbed my Aaron's hand. He gave no resistance as I pulled him to the door.

"So, Aaron Miller, you want to tell me what this is all about?"

He sighed. "Pops has a fondness for the fruit of the vine."

"And how does a Mennonite develop that?"

He shrugged. "I suppose it had to do with Mom dying. One of his farming buddies must have brought him a little homemade something to help ease the pain. I guess he liked it."

"Must have been a Presbyterian," I said.

"What?"

"Never mind. So, you were going to have your father move in with us and not tell me he has a drinking problem?"

"He doesn't have a drinking problem. And I would have told you, sooner or later. It's just that Pops is very sensitive on the subject. You know how we Mennonites are. And anyway, with all our wedding plans, and then finding Sarah, I just forgot."

It was possible that he forgot. Just the week before I'd spent nearly an hour searching for my car keys when they were in my hand the entire time. And I did indeed understand how he might be reluctant to tell me such a thing, given that I am a fairly staunch Mennonite. By today's standards at least.

I mean, not only do we eschew drunkenness but we perceive alcohol itself as being somehow inherently evil. Mama always said that you could tell if someone drank just by looking at the veins in their wrists. According to her, imbibers and true believers had visibly different vascular systems. Of course, now I know it isn't true, but for years I would glance discreetly up the cuffs of our non-Mennonite friends, trying to tell the teetotalers apart from the sinners.

"I believe in complete honesty between us," Aaron added. "You do believe that, don't you?"

I nodded vigorously. I felt so ashamed for having fantasized that my Pooky Bear was a mass murderer that I was willing to believe anything he said.

"Of course I believe you, Aaron. Tell me anything, and I'll believe it."

"Okay," Aaron said. He took a deep breath. "Try this on for size. I just got back from Beechy Grove Mennonite church. You won't believe what the grave digger found while digging Sarah's grave."

"What?" I asked calmly.

"Her mother."

I didn't believe him.

24

"That isn't funny, Aaron."

He wasn't smiling. "And I'm not joking. Sarah's gravesite is in the family plot, which, as you can imagine, has gotten rather full over the years. Anyway, the guys digging Sarah's grave hit something only three feet down. I hate to say this, but those guys aren't too bright. At first they thought it was cow bones—because they weren't in a coffin, or even a box. Then one of the guys found the skull. Definitely human."

I squatted to blow the dust and hay away from the edge of Pops's pit. Then I sat down.

"What makes you think it was your Aunt Rebecca? Like you said, the plot is getting full. It may be someone else they uncovered. Maybe a headstone is missing."

Aaron sat down beside me, sharing the place I had cleared. "Well, I suppose we can't be one hundred percent sure that it is Auntie Rebecca until they compare dental records or something, but I'm sure."

"Why?"

"Because Pops is sure."

I turned and glanced up at my father-in-law-to-be. Why on earth would my Pooky Bear take the word of an old goat who had defied his religion and built a secret wine cellar in his barn? The fact that the old goat was his father didn't count. My father told me that he had once seen a large disk—about half the size of a football field—hover over our north pasture, and I hadn't believed him. Come to think of it, Papa and Aaron Senior had been best buddies and seemed to spend a lot of time in this very barn.

"Why are you so sure, Pops?" I asked gently.

Pops joined us, sitting on the edge of the little cellar. That left only Uncle Elias standing, not that you could tell it by our relative heights.

"They found a brace buried with her. I saw it. It was hers."

"Your sister wore braces?"

"Not on her teeth. On her leg. Becca had polio when she was a kid. The doctors said she'd never walk again, but she showed them."

I shook my head in wonder. "I didn't know her very well, but I never noticed."

"She got to where she barely limped," Pops said. "And she always wore her skirts long."

I told Pops how sorry I was that his sister's death had been confirmed. He appreciated my sentiments, and he seemed to be taking it all pretty well. After all, Becca had disappeared twenty years ago, so Pops had had a chance to adjust to the idea that she was probably dead. But seeing her bones and her brace had to have been awfully hard on him, so I waited as long as I could before voicing what was on my mind.

At last I took a deep breath. "So, what does this do to the plans for Sarah's funeral this afternoon?"

"Ah, that," my Aaron said. "I'm afraid that depends on Jonas."

"What?"

"Jonas was there, of course. At the cemetery. We called him from the church. He wants to postpone Sarah's funeral until after the coroner has made a positive ID and Melvin has released the remains. Jonas's idea is to have a double funeral. Pops told him that we should just leave Auntie Rebecca where she is and have a combination memorial-funeral service this afternoon, but of course that isn't an option."

"Why not?" I wailed.

He put his arm around me. "Procedures have to be followed. The state has certain requirements for burials."

"But why disturb someone after twenty years?"

"And they don't need to do any tests on her either," Pops said, his voice choking. "I know without a doubt that's my kid sister."

Aaron put his other arm around his father. "Don't worry, Pops. I'll see to it that this gets settled as quickly and simply as possible. I have a friend in the DA's office in Harrisburg who owes me a favor from when we were in 'Nam. He might know someone who can help speed things along. Melvin sure the hell doesn't."

"Melvin couldn't find his way out of a paper bag if the directions were printed on the inside," I said charitably.

"It looks to me like Melvin isn't the only problem here," Uncle Elias said quietly. "I think someone ought to talk to Jonas."

"I will," I volunteered.

My Pooky Bear's arm squeezed tighter around my shoulders. "Let someone else do it. You've got enough to do."

"Like what"

"Like take a bath, for instance."

"Why, I never!" I flung Aaron's arm off and stood up.

"I was just kidding," he said quickly. "I only meant that since the Hernia jail doesn't have a bathtub—"

I was out of there. I don't think I'd ever been so insulted. I shower every day and use a deodorant- antiperspirant, and I do not smell. Okay, so my overnight stay in jail may have ripened me up a little bit, but not enough for anyone else to notice. I barely had. And how did Aaron know what the bathing facilities were like in the Hernia jail?

Even though I hoofed it home, I was still fuming when I got to my front drive. I was certainly in no mood to have Auntie Vonnie ambush me from behind a sugar maple.

"It's a shame how you let this place get run down, Magdalena."

I kept walking.

"Why, just look at your yard. It's full of dandelions. My yard in Fox Chapel doesn't have a single dandelion. My gardener would never permit it. Why don't you do something about yours?"

"This is a farm, dear," I said patiently. "Weeds happen."

"And those wild onions—"

I stopped. "I'm sure you've heard the latest news, Auntie Vonnie. Haven't you?"

She looked me right in the eye. "Of course I have. Jonas stopped by on his way back into town. What a shame."

I couldn't believe my ears. "That's it? A shame? Two men find the remains of your sister this morning—after twenty years—and all you have to say is it's a shame? It's a shame like the dandelions are a shame?"

"Well, of course I'm devastated. But like you said, it happened twenty years ago. That's a long time to get used to the idea."

"Get used to what?" I nearly shouted. "No one knew for sure what happened until this morning. And we won't know any of the details until after the investigation. If it was my sister, Susannah—"

"Investigation. What kind of investigation?"

"I don't mean to be unkind, dear," I said patiently, "but your sister was murdered. I mean, she didn't dig her own grave, now did she?"

"Well, you don't have to be so cruel," Auntie Vonnie snapped. She stomped off like a draft horse trying to dodge gnats. I hoped she was stamping on dandelions and wild onions, which were indeed becoming an eyesore.

I went in to barricade myself in my bedroom and run the bath my beloved had badgered me into taking. But before that I stopped by the kitchen to see Freni.

"How about we serve a wilted dandelion salad for lunch?" I suggested sweetly.

Freni frowned. "I already made a tossed salad with that iceberg lettuce the English like so well."

"Well, it was just a thought. Anyway, the aunties have become so citified that they've probably forgotten how good a wilted dandelion salad can taste. Chances are they wouldn't like it."

Freni brightened. "On the other hand, those new zippered storage bags you bought will keep the lettuce fresh for days. And it's best to eat dandelion greens as early in the season as possible. I'll see what I can do."

I went happily to my bath.

True, showers are more hygienic than baths are, but the latter are more therapeutic. And since Susannah has enough bath oils and bubble-producing brews to last a harem their collective lifetimes, I borrowed a not-so-subtle fragrance called Midnight Pleasures. If Aaron thought I smelled bad before my bath, just let him get a whiff of me after it.

To my delight, Midnight Pleasures produced enough bubbles to bury a small city, and I will admit that I had a great time playing in the tub. In fact, not since a babysitter from our church let me and a neighbor boy, Andrew, bathe together when we were five have I had so much fun surrounded by porcelain.

Unfortunately, Mama came home while Andrew and I were having our bath and read our babysitter the riot act. Two children, of different sexes, bathing in the same water! According to Mama, the gates of hell had all but opened to receive the wicked woman.

Rumor has it that the poor woman—who still attends my church—was so traumatized by Mama's tongue-lashing that she has never touched, a tub since, only showers. To this day she can't look me in the eye without blushing. As for Andrew, thank goodness he's off living in San Francisco, so I am seldom reminded of that shameful incident.

At any rate, I was busy sculpting a soap bubble castle when I distinctly heard someone say my name. Being the religious sort, and being alone in my bathtub, I just assumed it was God. Who else would speak to me under those circumstances?

"Yes, Lord," I said reverently. Of course I wasn't frightened. You wouldn't be either, if you had my background.

"No need to call me that," the Lord said. He had a distinctly feminine voice. A familiar voice, in fact.

I scooped a foam turret aside and gazed with horror upon a face. It belonged to Diane Lefcourt, however, not the Lord. She was wearing a pastel floral dress and virtually no makeup. She looked almost normal.

"What are you doing here?" I shouted. Then I remembered to cover strategic parts of my chest. The foam enhanced, rather than hid, my meager holdings, but I was too angry to be pleased with the discovery. "So? Who let you in?"

Diane smiled wickedly. "I worked in a carnival, remember? I could pick my way into Fort Knox if I wanted to, only this time I didn't need to pick any locks. That old lady with the bonnet did it for me."

"Freni?"

"What that woman can do with a hairpin! She could be rich working the better suburbs of Johnstown."

"Freni!"

"Shhhh! It's not her fault. I told her I was here on business. That I was a florist here to check on the delivery for your wedding Saturday."

"You didn't! You're lucky Freni didn't recognize you. She's not very fond of you. And how did you know I'm getting married Saturday?"

"The newspaper, how else? After you left yesterday, I remembered seeing your face somewhere. It's a bit unusual, you know. Anyway, I dug through a stack of old papers and there you were. Your engagement announcement."

"Why are you really here?" I asked. "And speak quickly," I added. What remained of my foam castle was rapidly deteriorating.

"I came for the funeral. Sarah's. I came early, to see you, because we need to talk."

"I don't understand, dear," I said. "Yesterday you told me that Becca was alive and in Harrisburg. Why would you come to her funeral?"

Diane Lefcourt's bottom lip began to quiver. "Of course I lied about Rebecca being in Harrisburg. I knew she couldn't be alive—not after all these years. Not without getting in touch with me. I told you she was in Harrisburg because I hoped you would go there looking for her. You see, I didn't trust you, and I wanted to throw you off the scent."

"What scent?" I had become particularly sensitive to that word.

"I didn't want you interfering in my business."

"I don't conjure up spirits," I said drily.

She shook her head vigorously. "Not that. The business of revenge."

"I don't do revenge either, dear. Please get to the point."

"I loved Becca Weaver. Like a sister. When I read in the paper that little Sarah had been found, I knew he would be here. To cover his tracks, if nothing else."

"Who are you talking about?"

She clucked impatiently. "Jonas. Who else?"

"You think Jonas killed his wife? And then his own daughter?"

"She wasn't his," she said softly.

"What?"

"Sarah. She wasn't Jonas's. He's sterile."

I didn't know whether to cover my ears or have her repeat it. "Huh?"

She repeated it.

"Who on earth told you such a thing?" I demanded.

"Becca told me. I said we were like sisters. She told me everything. She told me Jonas shot blanks on account of a bicycle accident when he was a boy."

"Now I am confused," I said.

"It's a figure of speech," she explained. "What matters is that he was not little Sarah's biological father."

"My Aaron's auntie an adulteress?" I moaned.

"Becca wasn't the saint everyone thought she was. Or we wouldn't have been friends." She laughed.

"Some things aren't funny, dear. Well, then, who was Sarah's father?"

She shrugged. "Becca never told me."

"I thought she told you everything," I said, perhaps meanly.

"She was afraid of what Jonas would do to the man if he found out. But I have an idea who the guy is, of course."

"Who?"

She had the nerve to give me a disapproving look. "Aren't we nosy, Magdalena Yoder?"

"I am not nosy!" I risked exposing myself by slapping the water with my hand for emphasis.

"Nosy or not," Diana said calmly, "I came here to talk about Jonas Weaver. It'll be a mockery to Becca's memory if he's allowed at little Sarah's funeral."

"Oh, you haven't heard," I said. I clamped a soapy hand over my mouth.

"Heard what?"

"Have a seat." I pointed to the toilet. "And look the other way while I grab a towel."

She laughed but did what she was told.

25

Magdalena Yoder's Wedding Feast, from Soup to Nuts

Auntie Lizzie's Mushroom and Pea Casserole

1 pound fresh mushrooms
2 tablespoons butter
1 8-ounce box frozen green peas, thawed
1 can cream of celery soup
¾ cup milk
1/8 teaspoon Worcestershire sauce
2 tablespoons grated Parmesan cheese
salt and pepper to taste
½ cup crushed potato chips

Wash and slice mushrooms. Saute in butter until lightly tender. Stir in peas and continue to cook for two minutes. Blend remaining ingredients (except for potato chips) and combine with mushrooms and peas. Pour mixture into well-greased baking dish. Sprinkle with potato chip crumbs. Bake 30 minutes at 350 degrees.

Serves 4-6.

26

Diane was plainly shaken by the news. It was a good thing she was sitting on the toilet. Unfortunately, she had misunderstood my invitation and was using the damn thing, an intimacy I am not accustomed to, I assure you. I kept my back turned until she flushed.

"That's all I know," I said. "Aaron's going to try and talk some sense into Jonas, but you know him."

"Yes, and the man's a monster." She began to cry. "Someone ought to do to him what he did to my Becca and her little Sarah."

"Well, if we can prove his guilt, the state will do it, and even if we can't, he'll get his just reward someday."

"Don't give me that crap," she sobbed. "I don't believe in religious mumbo jumbo."

I suppose we are all entitled to our own beliefs— or the lack thereof—but for someone who tried to pass herself off as both a nun and King Tut, she was in need of a little spiritual guidance.

"Read your Bible, dear. There is going to be a day of reckoning, and whoever killed these two is going to have to answer to God."

She grabbed a hand towel, without washing her hands, and dabbed at her face. Apparently she hadn't heard a word I'd said.

"Jonas Weaver is not going to get away with this," she said through gritted teeth. "That man is going to pay."

"Wash your hands," I said gently. "Cleanliness is next to godliness, and on both counts you seem to be way out in the north pasture."

She did what she was told, which was fortunate, because, without being invited, she stayed for lunch.

Lunch began as a disaster and I would rather not go into all the details. Suffice it to say, Freni might not have recognized the infamous Diane Lefcourt after all these years, but the other women sure did. They carried on like hens when a fox has invaded the coop. Aaron and Pops had not shown up, so presumably they were still trying to talk sense into Jonas. If it hadn't been for the fact that Freni's wilted dandelion salad slipped by them not only undetected but much appreciated, I would have fled back to my tub.

Auntie Vonnie seemed especially fond of the greens. "Endive this good can come from only one place. The Giant Eagle in Fox Chapel, right?"

I nodded, which isn't the same as lying, because in some cultures it means no.

"Ach, no," said Freni, who had come in to refill the bowl. "Those are dandelions from the yard. Frankly, it's a little late in the year, and some of the leaves are a little tough if you ask me."

I flashed daggers at her, but the woman has all the sensitivity of sandstone.

"They would look better, too, but something seems to have stepped on them. Maybe one of the cows got loose last night. I'll have to ask Mose."

While I prayed that the good Lord would get me safely out of that one, I stabbed at the ice in my water glass. Freni insists on filling glasses with the ice already in them, which is the surest way of making those damn cubes stick together.

Apparently the Lord heard my silent prayers for deliverance because the two Aarons appeared suddenly in the door. All eyes turned to them.

The younger Aaron shook his handsome head. "That man is as stubborn as—as—"

"As sin," I said. I passed the serving bowls down to their places while they took their seats.

Instead of picking up his fork, my Pooky Bear slammed his fist down on the table. "He just won't listen to reason! Legally he might be Auntie Rebecca's next of kin, but he isn't the only kin she had. There's all of you."

"And you," I pointed out.

"That's right," Pops said. "We're her family too. More so than Jonas, if you ask me. Becca was my baby sister, my flesh and blood."

"But Sarah was his flesh and blood," Auntie Lizzie said, her loyalties perfectly obvious.

I bit my tongue and cast Diane a warning look. The water was choppy enough. We certainly didn't need any boat rocking.

She spoke up nonetheless. "Well, you could have your own service. Not a funeral maybe, but a memorial service. For the two of them. I mean, you do have the church reserved for three this afternoon."

I breathed a sigh of relief. Everyone else turned and stared at her.

Frankly, I thought it was a brilliant idea. Face it, what did it really matter if the Weaver women's remains were not actually there at the service? They wouldn't care. They weren't inhabiting those bones any longer. A memorial service was intended for the living, and with the exception of one stubborn old man, all the living relatives were gathered around my dining room table. Susannah, of course, was at work, but she had scheduled to take off at two and was planning to show up at the church.

"It's a great idea," I said.

"It has some merit," Auntie Vonnie said, much to my surprise.

Uncle Rudy just rudely got up from the table, without being excused, and wandered off.

Uncle Elias gave the thumbs-up sign, while Auntie Magdalena whimpered her consent.

Auntie Leah boomed her approval and Uncle Sol, not to be outdone, bellowed his. I was almost surprised to hear he had a voice.

Only Auntie Lizzie and Uncle Manasses remained holdouts.

"Jonas was a part of this family long before you were even born," she said, looking at me as if the whole situation were somehow my fault. "And you're not even part of the family yet."

"Well, I've been a part of this family longer than any of you," Aunt Vonnie snapped, "and I say we go ahead and have the service. Put it all behind us, except for the actual interment, of course. It's time we get on with things."

I couldn't believe my ears. Freni must have mixed some jimsonweed in with the dandelion leaves. Either Auntie Vonnie was suffering from delirium or I was.

"I guess that settles it, then," said my Aaron. Although he was the youngest blood relative there, he seemed the one most capable of making decisions. I was immensely proud of him.

"Three o'clock it is," Pops said. You could hear the sadness in his voice. "You know, it's really too bad that Jonas has to act this way. And after what I did for him today too."

"What did you do for him, Pops?" I asked gently. "Take him some liquid refreshment?"

It just slipped out, honest. I would never rat on my soon-to-be-father-in-law. Not with my Pooky Bear present. I didn't deserve the looks that both Aarons cast my way. Uncle Elias too, come to think of it.

"Well, what did you do?" Diane Lefcourt was like a dog, worrying at all the bones I left in my wake.

Pops rubbed at the condensation on his water glass with a pumice-like thumb. "When Aaron and I went to see him, I dropped off some old letters I'd been keeping."

"What kind of letters?" I beat King Tut to the punch.

"Letters from Becca, to my Catherine. I thought it might soften him up a bit."

"Pops keeps everything," Aaron said quickly. "You should see his attic."

He was right, and it wasn't just the attic. The Miller house gave a new definition to the word clutter. Pops saved everything. Even soap slivers. True, his compulsion did save on housework—it was impossible to clean in there—but it made for a bizarre lifestyle. It was no wonder that the man sent over a barrel of sauerkraut twenty years old. Whatever Pops planned to do with all his stuff...

I recoiled in horror. "Two small suitcases and a garment bag," I said firmly. "And when the soap gets thin enough to see through, out it goes."

Before Pops could agree, Diane the dog picked up another one of my bones. "What was in those letters, Aaron?"

He shrugged his thin shoulders. "I don't know. I don't know if I even ever read them. I saw them the other day along with some of my Catherine's things." He looked around at the group, a spark igniting in his eyes. "I wouldn't have given them to that fool, except that I thought it might help."

My Pooky Bear reached over and lovingly patted his father's arm. "Don't worry, Pops. I'm sure you did the right thing. You did what Mama would have wanted."

There was a chorus of concurring voices, but other than that we finished our meal in silence. We were all undoubtedly deep into our own little worlds. I know I was.

I told Freni to stack the dishes and take the rest of the day off. She reminded me that she had been planning to do just that anyway. After all, she had known Auntie Rebecca all her life, living just down the road as she did, and she had been the one to discover Sarah in the barrel of kraut. She had fully intended to be at the funeral and still intended to be present at the memorial service. Mose would be there as well.

Taking care not to be seen by anyone, I dashed off to my room to change my dress. Black is the only appropriate color for a funeral—or memorial service—if you ask me. All right, dark gray will do, but only if it's so dark you can't find a pencil lead in your lap. Last summer, at Millie Neubrander's funeral, some woman from Philadelphia (an Episcopalian!) showed up wearing a bright-red sleeveless dress. It was an open-casket funeral, and there were those sitting in the front row who claim that Millie sat up in her coffin, a look of abject horror on her face. Of course I don't believe that, but even from where I was sitting I could see the coffin shudder. I know I did.

Anyway, I hurriedly dressed and then carefully sneaked out of my room and out of the inn. I had a very important errand to perform. Before we laid Sarah and her mother to rest in our hearts, there was something equally as important that needed to be laid to rest.

Some way or another, I was going to make that horrid little Jonas Weaver confess to what he had done. That he was guilty I had no doubt. It was plain as day what had happened. When that slimy snake— who had only been shooting blanks, as Diane said— found out many years after the fact that his wife had cheated on him, he killed her. Then, when he learned that Sarah—who was not his biological daughter— had witnessed the heinous crime, he killed her too.

While it was not in my province to mete out justice to Jonas, I was fully within my rights to see that he owned up to his crimes. He had single-handedly ruined my wedding week and caused me immeasurable grief.

Of course the paring knife I'd smuggled out of the kitchen was intended only for my protection. The pocket-size tape recorder, however, I planned to use. By hook or by crook, I would trap that spawn of Satan into making a confession. By Saturday morning Jonas Weaver was going to be behind bars.

27

Delores lives on the kind of street Norman Rockwell liked to paint. Granted, hers is a rooming house, but the rest of the homes are single-family abodes, many of them decked out in genuine Victorian gingerbread. Huge maples line both sides of the street, and in just about every other yard stands a majestic Colorado blue spruce. Wherever enough sunlight gets through, someone has scratched out a flower bed. It is a street of shady solitude, where the only discordant sound is the occasional whine of electric hedge shears.

It was precisely 1:16 when I parked my car. I am positive of the time because I purposely looked at my watch. Being late to a funeral—or a memorial service—is almost as bad as wearing red. If the dead can make it there on time, why can't the mourners?

Of course I wasn't dumb enough to park right in front of Delores's rooming house. I might not know everyone in Hernia, but it's a sure bet everyone knows me. On the off-chance that some disgruntled soul would recognize my car and pop in to settle an old score during my tete-a-tete, I parked all the way on the other side of the block. It took me six minutes to walk to Delores's, and I will confess that I was slightly out of breath when I rang the bell.

Although Delores's car was in her driveway, she didn't answer. I know for a fact that the woman, on account of her hearing problem, has lights in strategic rooms that come on whenever her doorbell is activated. I also know that she is as stubborn as a knot in a wet shoelace and is quite capable of just ignoring the world when it suits her to do so. Undoubtedly she was somewhere inside, peeking through the curtains and having herself a good laugh at my expense. It was also quite possible that Jonas was there as well and the two of them were busily engaged in doing the hootchie-cootchie—as Susannah so crudely puts it.

There was nothing left for me to do but to try the front door. It was locked. Ditto for the back door. But as they say, the third time is the charm—the side door that opens onto the breezeway and the garage was not locked. I slipped in quietly. Let me assure you that the purpose of my stealth at that point was to catch Jonas alone if possible. If I had been up to nefarious purposes I certainly would not have rung the doorbell.

A short flight of steps led up from the side door to the back hall, and I had just mounted the last one when the lights went out. I'm not talking about the hall light either, but the light in my head. It was as if someone had flipped a switch or pulled a chain. One minute I could see relatively fine (Delores is a tightwad and uses low-wattage bulbs); the next thing I knew, everything was as black as sin.

When the light in my head came on again, it brought a rush of intense pain. I can only describe it as hitting your head hard up against a wall while suffering a migraine and listening to rap music full blast on a boom box. And I'll throw in an off-key opera singer, a couple of mating cats, and some fingernails scraping across a chalkboard just to make sure I haven't understated the discomfort. If I could have gotten up and walked away from my head at that moment, I would have. Unfortunately, it was still firmly connected to my body.

For the first few minutes after the lights came on, there was no picture. Just sound. Gradually I got a fuzzy picture, then some double images, and finally what might pass for normal vision, except that every movement I observed was somehow connected to sound. The reverse seemed to be true as well.

"Magdalena, are you all right?"

The lights flickered on and off with every word, but I recognized Diane Lefcourt. She was sitting across from me in a chair. She appeared to be tied to it. I was likewise sitting, but at the moment I couldn't feel anything but my head. I may have been tied as well.

"No, I am not all right!" Each word was like hitting myself on the head with a hammer.

"Just sit real still then and keep your eyes closed."

Given my condition, that was easier done than said, and so I did it. I closed my eyes and sat there, willing the pain to go away. I have been told that I am a woman of strong character, but the truth is, it's my constitution that is remarkable. It is all in my genes. If Mama and Papa hadn't met an untimely end between the milk tanker and the shoe truck, chances are they would have survived well into their nineties. Neither of them ever had the patience to be sick, and I seem to have followed in their footsteps.

Perhaps five minutes had passed when I opened my eyes again. I felt much better. I could see quite clearly now, and the rap music and screeching soprano had been replaced by nothing more than a slight buzzing in my ears and a world-class headache.

I looked around the room. We were in a small back bedroom on the second floor. No, make that a tiny bedroom on the third floor, front side, up under the eaves. Through the one small window I could see the top levels of the maples that lined the street. The cubicle was furnished with a double bed, which took up most of the room, and a chair. I was sitting sideways on the bed, which had no headboard, and my hands were tied behind me. My feet, which were also tied together, stuck straight out in front of me. There was a rope around my waist, and behind me I could feel the sharp, cold metal ribs of an old-fashioned steam radiator. It was a good thing it was summer and the heat wasn't on.

Diane sat on a chair facing the bed. It had four legs, but one of them was much shorter than the other, and the slightest movement caused her to tip forward. Fortunately her center of gravity was well to the back of the chair, so she was in no danger of falling over. But the near constant jarring of that short leg against the floor, and her pitiful yelps and gasps were most annoying. She was undoubtedly responsible for some of the sounds I had heard in my altered state.

"What on earth are you doing here?" I was finally able to ask, with only minimal pain.

She rocked forward, gasping needlessly. "I came to see Jonas, which is undoubtedly what you did."

I nodded, which was stupid of me and very painful. "How long have you been here?"

"I don't know. I left right after lunch, so I guess I arrived about twenty minutes before you did."

"It took me a good bit more than twenty minutes to wash the dishes and change my dress, dear," I said, perhaps a bit crossly.

"Well, okay, then," she snapped. "I stopped off at a store. I had some shopping to do."

"In Hernia?"

"Miller's Feed Store. Look Magdalena, you and I both came here for the same reason, right? So let's stop playing games and lay our cards on the table. How were you planning to do him in?"

"What?"

"I thought of shooting him, but I don't have a gun, and that waiting period is just ridiculous, if you ask me. Of course I couldn't poison him, not unless I had him over to dinner, and the Sisters of the Broken Heart would never allow that. Not even a male pheromone is allowed past that gate. So I took a cue from you."

"What?"

"You know, at lunch you were stabbing at that clump of ice in your glass, and I got to thinking, what better way than an ice pick? I mean, it is summer, and everyone has an ice pick, right? I could stab Jonas with the pick—a couple of times if I needed to—wash it off good, and throw it along the road-side on my way home. They could never trace something that common back to me. So, I made a quick detour to Miller's Feed Store and—"

"Feed stores carry ice picks?"

She laughed and the chair rocked precariously. "Industrial-strength ice picks. One jab would have done it. Right in the eyeball."

I shuddered, which didn't do my headache any good. "That's horrible. I can't believe you were going to do that."

"And you, Little Miss Perfect? What were you going to do? From what I heard, you got caught with a tape recorder and a butcher knife. What were you going to do, carve him up and record his screams?"

I couldn't believe that even a fake nun would talk like that. It had to be the influence of television. The devil in a box, Mama used to call it.

"It was a paring knife, not a butcher knife. And it was for self-defense purposes only."

"I thought you Mennonites were pacifists," she said cruelly.

"But I'm supposed to get married on Saturday," I wailed. "I can't afford to get killed!"

The cubicle door opened. "What the hell—so, I see you're awake."

"Uncle Rudy! Am I ever glad to see you! You wouldn't believe—"

"Shut up." Uncle Rudy waved a small handgun in my general direction.

"Yes," I whispered, "I should keep it down. We don't want Uncle Jonas to know you're here. How did you find us?"

Diane Lefcourt brayed like a banshee. It took me a moment to recognize that it was laughter.

"Shut up, bitch!" Uncle Rudy growled.

It was a good thing I was sitting, because I would have hit the floor for sure. As it was, the shock gave me a permanent gray streak along my left temple. Fortunately it is a very narrow streak and I am able to blend it in with the rest of my hair.

"Uncle Rudy!" I gasped.

His face had turned into a smooth, hard mask. I could no longer recognize the meek little uncle who slept his days away on my parlor settee.

"Goddamn you, Magdalena."

Sometimes I'm as slow as molasses during a January cold snap. "But I thought you were Uncle Jonas. I mean, I thought Uncle Jonas did this to me—conked me on the head and tied me up. Where is Uncle Jonas? And Delores?"

He snorted. "Trussed up like turkeys one floor below you. Just like you two."

"And you're a pig, Rudy," Diane said defiantly.

"I said shut up, bitch!" Uncle Rudy turned and waved the pistol menacingly in front of her face.

The braying stopped. "Make me!"

There was the sound of metal hitting flesh. A dull thunk, not unlike when Freni tenderizes flank steak with a stainless-steel mallet. Diane slumped silently in her chair.

I screamed. I would like to say that I did it to draw attention away from Diane, but the truth is I was horrified. I have never been struck, much less with a pistol. Then again, given the size of my headache, perhaps I had been.

"You," I said through gritted teeth, "you killed Auntie Rebecca and Sarah?"

He turned toward me, waving the bloody pistol. For a second I thought I would be next. But Uncle Rudy has short arms, and I was sitting across the bed. It soon became clear to both of us that he wouldn't be able to strike me in the face—not without climbing across the bed. Call me a fool, but I didn't think he had it in him to shoot me head on. Not with me staring him in the eye. Bashing skulls seemed to be his MO.

"Why?" I cried. "Just tell me why. They were your relatives, for Pete's sake!"

"Goddamn you, Magdalena, why couldn't you mind your own business?"

"Sarah turned up in a wedding present!" I screamed. "She is my business."

He was sweating profusely, and with his free hand ripped his tie loose. "Sarah wasn't supposed to be involved. She saw something she shouldn't have. I couldn't help it. I had to silence her."

"By bashing her skull and stuffing her in a barrel of kraut?"

He wiped his forehead on a sleeve. "I would have buried her, but I didn't have time. Lucky for me the Millers had a bumper crop of cabbage that year and their root cellar was packed with barrels."

"But you killed her!" I was getting hoarse.

"It was her mother's fault," he whined. "She had a religious conversion and needed to cleanse her conscience. She was threatening to tell our little secret. She wanted to get it out in the open, have a full church confession. That sort of thing. And after all those years!"

"You're talking about Sarah being your daughter, aren't you?" Suddenly it all made sense.

The slits opened just wide enough for me to see that his eyes were indeed brown. "You know?"

"I do now. Up until now I only knew that Jonas wasn't Sarah's biological father. But I never suspected that her real father was one of her so-called uncles. Thanks for filling in the blanks."

"You're a real smart-ass, Yoder, you know that? Always sticking your nose in where it doesn't belong. Well, I'll soon take care of that. You like roast turkey, Yoder?"

"If it's the self-basting kind, and not too dry." I took a deep breath and shifted my brain into high gear. "Look, I came here hoping I could work something out with Uncle Jonas. Something legal. Maybe I could help you find a legal out. You know, if you turn yourself in, they might go easier on you."

"And her?" He jabbed a stubby thumb back at Diane. "What's her game?"

I shrugged as much as my ropes let me.

"Extortion, that's what!"

"But she—" Fortunately I stopped myself. Vengeance or extortion, it didn't matter right then.

"What?" he snarled.

"I was only going to say that I find it almost impossible to believe that a man could kill his own daughter. How could you, Uncle Rudy?"

"Shut up!"

There was a desperation in his voice that made me think the devil might have a conscience after all. "Well? She was your own flesh and blood, for Pete's sake."

"I told you, she saw something she wasn't supposed to see. She had to go. It was her or me."

"But why did you have to kill Auntie Rebecca in the first place? Would it have been so bad if she had told? Not that I approve, of course, but people have affairs all the time."

He mopped at his face with the loosened tie.

"Those were different times, Magdalena. I would have been booted out of the family, and I needed the money."

"What money?"

The polyester tie only smeared the sweat around. "My business was failing. You know, the Reagan recession. I needed Vonnie's income from the trust to keep it afloat."

"So Auntie Vonnie was your goose?"

He stared at me.

"That laid the golden eggs, I mean."

"Yeah, only the goose stopped laying, didn't it? But by then it didn't matter. My company suddenly took off in a big way. Who would have thought that little bits of plastic could make me a multimillionaire?"

"Auntie Vonnie must have," I said thinking aloud. It is a terrible habit of mine. Undoubtedly it comes from being the oldest child by ten years and playing alone on a farm.

Uncle Rudy sneered, revealing baby-size teeth. "You're a smart cookie, Magdalena. And so was Vonnie. She figured early on about my affair with Becca. Sarah had brown eyes like me. The rest of the bunch all have blue or green.

"But by then I had gotten a patent for my computer chips, and things were looking up for my company in a big way. Did you know that Gerber Electronics ranks number three internationally in computer software? Would you care to guess how many people I employ and what my company does for Pittsburgh's economy?"

I rolled my eyes. "Face it, Uncle Rudy. What's really important is that it pays for Auntie Vonnie's eight-thousand-square-foot house with the indoor pool and the four-car garage. That's what bought her silence."

"Vonnie loves me," he said pathetically.

"Yeah, like I love Shnookums."

"What the hell did you say?" His tone was ugly again. If I wasn't more careful, I was going to have to wear an extra-thick veil on my wedding day.

"I think we can still work something out, you know," I said quickly. "If Leona Helmsley could run an empire from jail, why can't you?"

He gave me the kind of look I usually reserve for Melvin. "Mine are capital offenses." He sounded almost proud.

"What about a temporary insanity plea? You know, say that you were under too much stress at the time."

"You watch too damn much TV," he growled. Little did he know. "Looks to me like I've only got one option."

"Turn yourself in and plead guilty?" I asked hopefully.

I'm sure he would have crawled across the bed and whacked me upside the head with the pistol if Diane hadn't moaned just then. Uncle Rudy jumped and whirled around, like a child playing hopscotch. It was all I could do to keep from snickering.

He examined Diane's ropes and turned back to me. Something about his eyes told me that in that brief moment I had lost all ground.

"I know you are a religious woman, Magdalena," he said coldly. "Prepare to die."

28

Believe it or not, I have heard those words—"prepare to die," or at least a variation of them—before. And believe it or not, I am prepared to die. I have every confidence in my salvation. Death holds no fear for me. It's how and when I die that concern me.

I smiled pleasantly. "You came to Hernia for my wedding, as well as for Sarah's funeral. You really should wait until you've had a chance to attend both. Freni is fixing a wedding feast that would be the envy of Cana—without the wine, of course."

"Doctor says I have to watch my cholesterol," he smirked, "and Freni's favorite dish is 'cholesterol casserole.'"

"Well, you should at least attend your daughter's funeral. It starts in less than an hour, and you don't want to be late. There will be plenty of time to kill me when you get back."

For some reason that amused him to the point that I got a second view of his tiny yellow teeth. "Oh, I'll be at that funeral all right. I'll be sitting right up there in the front row."

"And me?" I asked hopefully.

"You and the rest of the turkeys will be doing what turkeys are meant to do. You'll be roasting until you're a nice golden brown." He laughed again. "Of course, there's a good chance the oven will be too hot and you'll be burnt. To a crisp!"

"Stuff and nonsense," I said irritably. "Delores does not have an institutional-size oven. And if you ask me, that's no way to run a proper boarding house. You simply can't—"

"Shut it, Yoder. I didn't ask you. This"—he waved a stubby arm—"is going to be your oven. Only thing is,"—he made a pouting face—"you forgot to bring the spices with you. And what's a turkey without proper seasoning? I guess I'll just have to run downstairs and get some."

To my surprise he turned and left the room, slamming the door behind him. Perhaps he wasn't kidding.

"Don't forget the sage!" I shouted after him. "And take it easy on the salt. Sodium contributes to water retention, you know."

I struggled with my ropes, but it was futile. For one thing, the knots were not within reach of my fingers, and for another, Uncle Rudy had used nylon clothesline. Where he had managed to get yards of the stuff on the spur of the moment was beyond me. Then I remembered that Delores was too cheap to buy a clothes dryer, even too cheap to drive into Bedford and use a laundromat. "My sheets smell fresh, like sunshine," she once bragged to me. Now, thanks to the old gal's penny-pinching penchant, not only was I trussed like a turkey but I was about to buy the farm.

"Why me, Lord?" I said aloud.

"Ugh," the good Lord groaned.

"I beg your pardon?"

"Damn, my head hurts."

My mouth opened to apple-bobbing width while my battered brain slowly informed me that it wasn't the Lord who was speaking, but Diane Lefcourt. I had to hand it to the woman. She made a lousy King Tut, but she made up for it with her God imitations, unintentional though they might be. Of course, by that I mean only that her timing was impeccable; she didn't sound anything like God.

"Diane?"

"He gone?"

"Momentarily."

"What happened?"

"I forgot the salt."

"Huh?"

"Never mind. How do you feel?"

"Like a truck ran over my head, backed up, and ran over it again."

"Welcome to the club. How are your knots, dear?"

"Throbbing," she said crossly. "I just told you."

"Not those kind of knots, sweetie. I meant the kind on your ropes. Can you reach them?"

She fumbled for a few minutes, breathing heavily. "No."

"I can't reach mine either, but I have an idea. If you can turn your chair around, maybe I can untie them with my toes."

At the risk of sounding vain, I am rather good with my toes. They are almost as long and slender as my little finger. If I were to sit immodestly, I could play cat's cradle all by myself. When Susannah was a little girl and would torment me at the supper table, I sometimes yielded to temptation and extracted my revenge in the presence of Mama and Papa. They never saw me pinch Susannah with my toes, and the knife and fork I held in my hands made perfect alibis.

"What?" Diane croaked. "Your toes?"

"I went barefoot all the time as a kid. You wouldn't believe what I can do with my toes."

"You being kinky, Magdalena?"

There was no time to be offended. "Look, near as I can figure, Uncle Rudy plans to burn this dump down with us turkeys in it. Unless you don't mind being Thanksgiving dinner five months early, turn your chair around and let me give it a shot."

For a fairly small woman—her large caboose aside—Diane made a lot of noise turning that chair around. Anyone directly beneath us might reasonably have guessed that there was an elephant waltzing upstairs. I'm sure being tied to a chair and suffering from a possible concussion made the task a bit difficult, but still, it was no wonder the woman quit the carnival and took up channeling.

I stretched my toes out as far as I could, but the knots remained out of reach. "Lean back," I coaxed.

I'm sure she tried to cooperate, but she was apparently afraid to let her feet leave the floor. Undoubtedly her center of gravity had betrayed her once before.

"You're going to need to tip all the way over backwards, hon," I said encouragingly. "You'll be landing on the bed. It won't hurt."

"I'm sixty-five years old, Magdalena, and I don't take estrogen. If I hit the floor I could break a hip. Sisters of the Broken Heart has lousy insurance."

I sighed patiently. "If Uncle Rudy gets back up here before we get loose, you won't have to worry about a hip replacement. Tip over backwards or burn."

Diane Lefcourt bravely pushed off with her toes, and just as I'd predicted, the back of her chair smacked against the side of bed. She grunted, but otherwise seemed none the worse for wear.

"Scoot your hands up a little, dear, if you can," I said.

"I am not Houdini," she said testily.

I egged her on gently, and at last she managed to wiggle her hands up an inch or so. I had to admire even that small gain, because I am sure it put quite a stress on her shoulder blades. Clearly, she hadn't been a contortionist in the carnival.

Fortunately I don't wear hose or socks in the summer unless I have to. Many Amish women go barefoot at home during the warmer months, and it is a custom that both Susannah and I have chosen to follow. Of course I wear hose to church, but that's a "have to" situation. After my bath that morning, I had slipped into a pair of sandals, not planning to don "plastic leg casings," as Susannah calls hose, until the very last moment. At any rate, it was a simple matter for me to kick off my sandals. It was quite another for me to untie the knots.

"Ouch! You should trim your toenails more often," Diane complained loudly.

"Shhh!"

"But they're so long and sharp."

"Susannah has scars on her shins to prove it." It was hard to concentrate and talk at the same time.

"And they stink!"

"Well, I never! You were there when I bathed!"

"Ouch!"

The light pinch on the wrist I'd given her did not merit such a loud reaction. Fortunately the last knot on her wrists came undone and we were able to move quickly on to the other things. Diane was less skilled with her fingers than I was with my toes, but she did manage to untie my knots.

"Now what?" Perhaps it was her carnival training again, but the woman definitely had a hawker's voice.

"I'll sit back on the bed, pretending to be tied up. Fortunately the door opens to face the bed. The second he starts to open the door I'll make a noise so he looks my way. In the meantime you'll be hiding behind the door with the chair. When he opens the door, whack him over the head with it." I don't believe in violence, mind you, but turnabout is fair play.

"But I'm an old woman," Diane whined. "Why do I have to hit him with the chair?"

"Because if he sees you sitting on the bed, he'll be suspicious, that's why. And you don't expect me to knock him on the noggin with the bed, do you?"

She reluctantly agreed to my plan—and just in time too. The instant Uncle Rudy turned the knob I let out a loud wail. Unfortunately King Tut didn't seem to have the strength of even a mummy and couldn't lift the chair above shoulder level. Uncle Rudy was not about to stand stock-still and stare at me wail forever.

"Hit him anyway!" I hollered.

Even as the last word was coming out of my mouth I leaped on Aaron's evil uncle. In my mind's eye I saw it as a powerful, yet graceful act. I was a lioness leaping on her prey. Diane told me later that she thought I looked like a circus clown shot from a cannon.

What matters is that I connected with Uncle Rudy, as did Diane's chair. Despite my trim figure, I weigh more than Diane, and the force of my leap, combined with my body weight, exceeded that of her weight and the rather timid whack she administered to Uncle Rudy's back. The end result was that I ended up on top of Rudy, who ended up on top of the chair. This chain of events could have been disastrous for Diane, except that after delivering her pitiful blow she staggered sideways and safely out of the way. The upshot was that the chair broke another leg. So did Uncle Rudy.

For a moment I thought his fall had knocked him out, but it had merely winded him. Still, while he was catching his breath, I managed to extract the gun from his chubby little hand. Taking a cue from Susannah, I stowed it in the safest place I knew. Aaron has since told me that this is a very dangerous spot and that an accidental discharge might have sent a bullet straight through my heart. At any rate, the next thing I did was grab those chubby little hands and tie them tightly together with the clothesline. It was while I was working on his feet that Uncle Rudy regained his power of speech.

"Damn! I think my leg is broken!"

I ignored his profanity. "You all right, Diane?"

"Except that every bone in my body aches and my head feels like it's about to explode, I'm okay."

"Well, then shake a leg," I said pointedly. "We have a funeral to make."

Just outside the door we found a decorative hurricane lamp containing kerosene, a pile of rags, and some long matches. The rags were really pairs of Delores's cotton underwear, and they looked in perfectly good condition to me (although I couldn't believe she wore only a size eight!). Apparently Rudy, who was obviously in a hurry, had simply raided her panty drawer.

"He really was going to roast us alive," Diane said. She sounded shocked.

"He's a wicked, wicked man, dear, but he has a terrible memory. He brought everything but the spices."

We both laughed. That's when Uncle Rudy cut loose with a string of four-letter words that would make the Whore of Babylon blush.

"That does it!" I said.

A pair of Delores's size eights, and the panty hose I had brought in my dress pocket but had yet to put on made an effective gag indeed. That done, we hurried off to look for Uncle Jonas and Delores.

It was Diane who found the pair. They had been trussed like turkeys as well and stashed in the walk-in closet in Delores's bedroom. They had been more docile than we, and consequently had not been hit. They had, however, been gagged. Poor Delores was going to have to rewash all her panties. Still, other than a few raw spots where they had struggled against their ropes, they were both fit as fiddles.

"I told you I was innocent!" Uncle Jonas crowed.

"And I told you I didn't steal the diary!"

We hugged each other joyfully, which, given our similar genetic and religious backgrounds, is saying a lot. Inspired by our example, Diane and Delores hugged each other too. Unfortunately Delores's exuberance got a little out of hand and I saw Diane wince.

She touched her head gingerly. "Who would have thought it was Rudy?"

"Not me!" I said.

"Me either," Uncle Jonas said. "Not until he barged in here waving that pistol."

Delores draped a wrinkled brown arm around Uncle Jonas's shoulders. She had more liver spots than a leopard but obviously considered herself still in the game.

"Well, I knew Jonas had nothing to do with this from the beginning. I don't harbor criminals at my establishment."

I rolled my eyes but politely said nothing.

Much to his credit, Uncle Jonas casually shrugged off Delores's arm. "It was Rudy who stole the diary! Can you believe that? He was afraid something in there would incriminate him. But he was especially afraid of those letters Aaron dropped off this morning."

"Yes, the ones from Auntie Catherine to Auntie Rebecca." I patted his arm. "I'm so sorry, Uncle Jonas. About Auntie Rebecca, I mean. I know she passed on a long time ago, but the fact that they found her just this morning has got to be hard on you."

He gently patted the hand that was patting his arm, and I took the hint and withdrew it. "You know," he said, "now that we've got the real killer— all tied up, so to speak—I just want to put it all behind me. After a proper funeral, of course. It's time to get on with my life."

"Indeed," said Delores hopefully.

I glared at her, as did Diane.

"I only wish I hadn't been so stubborn and told the two Aarons to stuff it when they were here. We could at least have had Sarah's funeral this afternoon."

"We still could," I said, brightening. "You weren't supposed to know this, but we were going to go ahead and have a memorial service anyway. I don't see any reason why we can't turn that into a proper funeral for both."

"For both?" he asked. "Doesn't there have to be some sort of official investigation?"

"Well, like you said, we have the killer. It's worth giving it a shot. Delores, where's your phone?"

Delores pointed. "Melvin Stoltzfus will never agree to this, Magdalena."

"But it makes sense!" Diane declared.

"That's my point."

I started to dial. "I have my ways."

29

Sarah Weaver and her mother got the dignified burial they deserved late Wednesday afternoon.

That evening Jonas Weaver moved back into the PennDutch, desperate to escape the clutches of the vamp Delores. There was plenty of room now that the Gerbers had found other quarters—behind bars.

Thursday and Friday passed in a blur. There were a million wedding details to be completed, but fortunately my soon-to-be family pitched in and helped where they could.

Freni and Auntie Leah buried the hatchet and settled into a marathon cooking spree. Altogether two hundred and fifteen people had responded affirmatively to the post-wedding buffet dinner, but the two women got carried away and made enough food to feed three hundred—Mennonites, that is. Since a fair number of the guests were from other denominations, there was really enough food for four hundred.

Auntie Lizzie never did apologize for her cutting remarks, but given her exquisite taste, I was thrilled when she volunteered to oversee the decorations. She recruited Aaron, who was a basket of nerves, and together they constructed a spectacular ribbon and floral gazebo in the side yard away from the barn.

In all modesty, I have to say that Hernia had never seen the likes of anything this grand.

Auntie Magdalena had no obvious talents, so I assigned her to housework. Unfortunately she had no talent there either, and Mama, with her white-glove test, would have been appalled with the results. Fortunately the reception was going to be outside. If any of the guests needed to relieve themselves, there was always the cornfield.

As for the uncles, as long as they napped in the parlor, we left them alone.

Thank goodness Susannah loved her job. She had taken off work for Sarah's funeral, but the next morning was right back at it again. If she kept it up, she was bound to get an actual paycheck—her first. If that kept up, she might have to start paying taxes. Who knew, someday she might even move out on her own. The possibilities that life dangled before her were endless, and all because she had a way with colors.

"I'm really good at it, Mags," she said proudly to me. It was Friday night, after the rehearsal dinner, and I was just about to hop into bed and will myself to sleep.

"That's nice."

"No, I mean I'm really good. I won first prize in a contest they were running at work."

"That's wonderful, dear," I said kindly. "You can tell me all about it tomorrow."

"But you're getting married tomorrow," she whined. "Let me tell you about it now."

I sighed. So what was a few minutes less sleep? I probably wasn't going to sleep a wink anyway. I may as well be nice to my sister one last time as a single woman. Come tomorrow I would be a married woman, a matron. And not only that, I would be married to the most handsome man in six counties. I could afford to be generous.

"Do tell, dear."

Susannah's eyes glowed. "It's your wedding present, Mags."

"What is?"

"What I won in the contest. You're going to love it!"

"You won a Porsche?"

She laughed gaily. "Don't be so silly. I won a color book for you."

"But I have a hard time staying between the lines," I said modestly.

"Mags, you're a hoot. I'm not talking about a coloring book; this is a color book. At Crazy Paints, Inc., a color book is like a new line. You know, one of those things that spreads out into a fan, with all the colors and their names on it."

"You named a color after me?" I was touched.

"No, silly, I won the right to name the entire book of colors after you. It's going to be called Magdalena Mania, and it will be available to distributors sometime this fall."

I was stunned. I have tried to be a big sister, but undoubtedly I've failed more times than I've succeeded. Still, I must have done something right in a major way for Susannah to honor me so. Mama and Papa would both be proud.

"Thanks, dear." I gave Susannah a quick squeeze. Neither of us likes to get mushy with the other.

She beamed. "I'm glad you like it, Mags. And you're going to love the colors, I know. Of course I haven't worked there long enough to be responsible for all their names, but some of the best ones are mine."

"Like what?" I asked. How easily I forget.

She hopped up on my bed and settled back against the headboard. "Let's see, there's Wrinkle White, Decay Gray—"

"What about Brutish blue?" I asked and whacked her with my pillow.

I finally fell asleep around three a.m. By then the first hundred sheep I had counted had multiplied to the point that they were about to overrun Australia. When I awoke, I thought I was still sleeping and in the middle of a bad dream. Real life, I knew, couldn't be that bad. It was raining!

And I don't mean drizzling, either. Or even just a nice steady rain. I mean a real frogstrangler. A gullywasher. I snapped on the radio.

"... and the good news is that Bedford County residents won't have to water their lawns this weekend." The announcer chuckled mercilessly. "The bad news is that you can expect this stalled front to remain in place until the early part of next week. Our forecast for this period calls for steady rain, locally heavy at times. There is a flash flood watch for low-lying areas. My advice, folks—he chuckled again— "is to build an ark. Don't say I didn't warn you!"

I snapped it off and peered out my bedroom window through the deluge. The ribbon and floral gazebo was in tatters. The ribbons hung in sodden clumps, the flower petals had long since washed away.

I turned my eyes heavenward. "Mama, Papa, do something!" I wailed.

Mama was always a fast worker, but I hadn't expected the phone to ring immediately.

"Magdalena, is that you?"

"Mama?"

"Don't be silly. This is Lodema Schrock, your pastor's wife. I'm afraid I have some bad news."

I clenched my free fist. "Spill it."

"Remember the wedding you were going to have here this afternoon?"

Who did she think I was, Melvin's identical twin sister? "Of course I remember. I'm the bride!"

"Yes, well, I'm afraid you're going to have to make other plans."

"If that skinny bucktoothed little windbag of a preacher has canceled my wedding for an afternoon of fly-fishing, he can cancel my membership," I shouted into the receiver. "And I tithe!"

It's true. I give ten percent of my considerable income to the church. But if Rev. Schrock thought tying a fly was more important than tying a knot, I would be happy to give that ten percent to some other worthy cause.

"Magdalena!" Lodema gasped.

"And another thing. You really should stick to the notes in the hymnal, dear. Last Sunday it sounded like a band of raccoons were scampering across that keyboard."

"Why, I never!"

"And neither will I," I wailed, "unless I get married this afternoon."

"Then quit feeling sorry for yourself and think of a way," Lodema snapped. "But whatever you do, let me know. If you're going to bail out, I'm not going to bother pressing Michael's suit pants until tomorrow morning."

"What? I thought the Reverend was off fly-fishing in West Virginia."

Lodema's laugh sounded like a fistful of jacks in a jelly jar. "It's raining there too. Michael's with the rest of the men, trying to get that tree off the church roof."

"What tree?"

"That old oak that used to stand between the church and the parsonage. All this rain was finally too much for it. It toppled over on the church about an hour ago." The jacks rattled again. "I would offer to let you use the parsonage, but that band of scampering raccoons you mentioned has messed it all up."

"I'm terribly sorry about that," I said quickly. I was, in fact. It is one thing to hold a reception for two hundred and fifteen people in one's yard, but it's quite another thing to cram that many into one's house. Not to mention that the Beeftrust was far messier than any band of raccoons.

"How sorry?"

I racked my brain. "Enough to buy your pineapple upside-down cake at the next bake sale."

It was the wrong answer. Actually, it was the right answer, badly put. Lodema Schrock can't give her cake away, a fact that has caused everyone in the women's fellowship a great deal of embarrassment.

"What I meant to say," I sputtered, "is that I would be delighted to buy your cake if no one else wants it."

She hung up.

I was married at 4:23 Saturday afternoon—in a barn. Because of the heavy rain only about fifty of the invited guests showed up. For the same reason, two uninvited guests showed up as well.

"Really, Mags," Susannah whined, "did you have to let the cows in? They're animals!"

I smiled bravely. "It's their home, dear. But speaking of animals, where's Shnookums?"

"Why, in my room, of course! I'm not a complete idiot, you know."

I was tempted to frisk her, and might have done so, if Diane Lefcourt hadn't started playing the introduction to "O Promise Me." Of course I don't keep a piano in my barn, but Diane, I learned, never travels anywhere without a harmonica. Apparently it was part of her act in the carnival.

Suddenly Barbara Hostetler's high soprano voice filled the air. Although the woman is certainly gifted, the acoustics in the barn left something to be desired. What would have sounded like the voice of an angel inside Beechy Grove Mennonite Church sounded instead like someone had stepped on Cyrus the cat. Freni, who was adjusting my veil, beamed.

"Shame on you, Freni," I chided her.

Freni rolled her eyes, an unbecoming gesture on someone well into their golden years.

"Remember," I whispered to Susannah, "as soon as she begins singing the second verse, you start walking up the aisle."

Susannah patted my arm in a rare show of sisterly affection. "That isn't an aisle, Mags. It's a hay- covered barn floor."

I patted her in return. "Then be careful and walk slowly. This hay is slippery."

Barbara began the second verse, and my baby sister dutifully set out for the far side of the barn, where Aaron, his father, and Rev. Schrock waited. I am pleased to report that, for one of the few times in her life, Susannah was wearing a proper dress—one that had been sewn together with stitches. While this may sound like a victory for my side, let me assure you this was a compromise. Black is not an appropriate color for weddings.

But then again, I suppose taste is in the eye of the beholder. There were those who advised me not to wear a full-length white bridal gown, on the grounds that I was of a "certain age." An off-white or cream suit, they said, was far more appropriate. But I defied them. It was my wedding after all, and I was only going to have this one.

The dress I chose would have made Princess Diana weep with envy, which is probably the real reason she stayed away. (Thanks anyway, for the sterling-silver escargot holders, Di.) My gown was white satin silk and floor length. The bodice was covered with literally hundreds of seed pearls, as was the hem of the full skirt. Under the skirt I had to wear three crinolines to give it shape. But my favorite thing of all was the train. It was an absolutely frivolous five yards of material, with no other purpose except to trail behind me, but it made me feel like a queen. Mama would never have permitted such an extravagance.

Then came the big moment, the one I had been waiting for my entire life. Diane, bless her soul, hit the first note of the wedding march loud and clear.

I took my first step down that makeshift aisle, the first step of the most important journey of my life. Why, then, Mama, didn't you somehow intervene and prevent me from planting the left heel of my new white pumps in a knothole on the barn floor? Was it because you were jealous of my happiness, Mama? Well, I hope it pleases you to know that what happened next was the most embarrassing moment of my life.

Even now it is too painful to remember in any detail. Suffice it to say that my pump remained put while I hurtled forward. Freni, always a fast thinker but not particularly knowledgeable about English fashions, stepped on my train to hold me back. Unfortunately the train was not detachable from the skirt, but the skirt was detachable from the bodice. I continued my forward movement with my top intact, but having shed my skirt easier than a snake sheds its skin. Thank the good Lord I was at least wearing the three crinolines.

Susannah heard me stumble and turned to help, but I waved her on. When faced with a situation like that, one has but two choices: find a hole large enough to crawl into or proceed with the greatest of dignity. Because the knothole was too small, I chose the latter. Aaron told me later that he had never been so proud of anyone or anything in his life. This supportive statement from my Pooky Bear almost made up for the rumors that have since circulated through the Mennonite grapevine that I got married in my skivvies. One particularly vicious wag way out in Indiana is supposed to have claimed that she saw me get married in the buff.

"Why, I never!" Lodema Schrock gasped loudly as I passed her seat.

"You wouldn't have the guts," Susannah said over her shoulder.

As for the good Reverend, he didn't as much as flicker an eyelash. Perhaps, as a man of the cloth, he had seen it all before, although quite probably his mind was off in West Virginia—fly-fishing. The service continued without any further hitches—until the next disaster.

"Into this holy union," Rev. Schrock intoned, "Magdalena Portulaca Yoder and Aaron Daniel Miller Jr. now come to be joined. If any of you can show just cause why they may not lawfully be married, speak now or else forever hold your peace."

The heavy barn door slid open with a thud and Auntie Leah burst in, accompanied by a gust of rain. In my excitement I hadn't noticed her absence.

"Someone left the cake out in the rain," she bellowed.

"I don't know if I can take it," I said, leaning heavily on Aaron's arm.

"Don't worry, hon," my Pooky Bear whispered. "When this is over I'm going to take you on the trip of your dreams—to Japan. It was going to be a surprise."

"Japan?" I was approaching a state of shock.

"What?" Auntie Leah barked.

Aaron turned to her and put a silencing finger to his lips.

"But it took so long to bake it," Auntie Leah boomed in despair, "and I won't have time to make that recipe again."

"Oh, no!" I wailed.

That's when Barbara Hostetler stepped forward. "Don't you worry, Magdalena. I have thirty pecan pies at home. You're welcome to them."

"Thirty pecan pies?" Delirium wasn't all that bad, as long as it solved your problems.

"Yah," Barbara said, with a smile that was clearly meant for Freni. "When I get my work done on the farm I spend my time baking pies for the English. John and I are saving up for our own place."

"Ach du lieber!" Freni started to pass out in her chair, but when Mose made no move to catch her, she sat up straight again.

"Well, then, may we continue?" Rev. Schrock asked. The edge to his voice hinted that he preferred grilled trout to pecan pie.

We nodded humbly.

"Magdalena Portulaca Yoder, will you have this man to be your husband, to live together in the covenant of marriage? Will you love him, comfort him, honor and keep him, in sickness and in health, and, forsaking all others, be faithful to him as long as you both shall live?"

"Ahooooooo!"

"I beg your pardon?"

I was staring helplessly at Susannah. It wasn't me who had yowled, but the bantam-size beast in her bra.

"She will," Susannah said, without skipping a beat.

Clearly Rev. Schrock was eager to get on with it. "And will you, Aaron Daniel Yoder, have this woman to be your wife, to live together in the covenant of marriage? Will you love her, comfort her, honor and keep her, in sickness and in health; and forsaking all others, be faithful to her as long as you both shall live?"

"I will," said my Pooky Bear loud and clear.

"Those whom God has joined together let no man put asunder," the reverend said quickly. "I now pronounce you man and wife. You may kiss the bride."

"Ahoooooo!" Shnookums yowled again.

This time everyone laughed.

Aaron grinned and put his arms around me. His lips met mine. I kissed my husband for the very first time.

30

Magdalena Yoder's Wedding Feast, from Soup to Nuts

Barbara Hostetler's Save-the-Day Pecan Pies

4 eggs, beaten
1 cup pecans, chopped
1 cup brown sugar
1½ cups dark corn syrup
½ cup melted butter
1 teaspoon vanilla
dash of salt
1 unbaked fluted piecrust

Preheat oven to 350 degrees. Combine all the filling ingredients and pour into the pie shell. Bake approximately 40 minutes or until set. Especially delicious when served slightly warm and topped with hand-cranked vanilla ice cream.

Serves 8.

DISCOVER TAMAR MYERS

An Amish Bed and Breakfast Mystery with Recipes Series (PennDutch)
Too Many Crooks Spoil the Broth
Parsley, Sage, Rosemary, and Crime
No Use Dying Over Spilled Milk
Just Plain Pickled to Death
Between a Wok and a Hard Place
Eat, Drink, and Be Wary
The Hand that Rocks the Ladle
The Crepes of Wrath
Gruel and Unusual Punishment
Custard's Last Stand
Thou Shalt Not Grill
Assault and Pepper
Grape Expectations
As the World Churns
Hell Hath No Curry
Batter Off Dead
Butter Safe than Sorry

Belgian Congo Mystery Series
The Witch Doctor's Wife
The Headhunter's Daugther
The Boy Who Stole the Leopard's Spots
The Girl Who Married an Eagle

Den of Antiquity Series
Larceny and Old Lace
Gilt by Association
The Ming and I
So Faux, So Good
Baroque and Desperate
Estate of Mind
A Penny Urned
Nightmare in Shining Armor
Splendor in the Glass
Tiles and Tribulation
Statue of Limitations
Monet Talks
The Cane Mutiny
Death of a Rug Lord
Poison Ivory
The Glass is Always Greener

Non-Series Books
Angels, Angels Everywhere
Criminal Appetites (anthology)
The Dark Side of Heaven

ABOUT THE AUTHOR

Tamar Myers was born and raised in the Belgian Congo (now just the Congo). Her parents were missionaries to a tribe which, at that time, were known as headhunters and used human skulls for drinking cups. Because of her pale blue eyes, Tamar's nickname was Ugly Eyes.

Her boarding school was two days away by truck, and sometimes it was necessary to wade through crocodile infested-waters to reach it. Other dangers she encountered as a child were cobras, deadly green mambas, and the voracious armies of driver ants that ate every animal (and human) that didn't get out of their way.

At sixteen, Tamar's family settled in America, and she immediately underwent culture shock: she didn't know how to dial a telephone, cross a street at a stoplight, or use a vending machine. She lucked out, however, by meeting her husband, Jeffrey, on her first day at an American high school. They literally bumped heads while he was leaving, and she entering, the Civics classroom.

In college Tamar began to submit novels for publication, but it took twenty-three years for her to get published. Persistence paid off, however, because Tamar is now the author of three ongoing mystery series: One is set in Amish Pennsylvania and features Magdalena Yoder, an Amish-Mennonite sleuth who runs a bed and breakfast inn; one, set in the Carolinas, centers around the adventures of Abigail Timberlake, who runs an antique and collectable store (the Den of Antiquity); and the third is set in the Africa of her youth, with its colorful, unique inhabitants.

Tamar now calls North Carolina home. She lives with her husband, a Basenji dog named Pagan, two rescue kitties: a very large Bengal named Nkashama, and an orange tabby cat who goes by the name of Dumpster Boy. Tamar enjoys gardening (she is a Master Gardner), bonsai, travel, painting and, of course, reading. She's currently working on her next Amish mystery.

tamarmyers.com